A Divine P

SINCERELY HERS

A Novel

By

Shenetta Marie

A Divine Production

ISBN 10: 0985149922
ISBN 13: 978-0985149925
Editor: Rubina Sardon
A Divine Production logo by: nicolejaneen@gmail.com
Cover Design by: Dynasty's Visionary Designs

Library of Congress Control Number: 2013900316

First Printing February 2013
Printed in the United States of America

10 9 8 7 6 5 4 3 2 1

This novel is a work of fiction. Any references to real people, event, establishments, or locals are intended only to give the fiction a sense of reality and authenticity. Other names, characters, and incidents occurring in the work are either the product of the author's imagination or are used fictitiously, as those fictionalized events and incidents that involve real persons. Any character that happens to share the name of a person who is an acquaintance of the author, past or present, is purely coincidental and is in no way intended to be an actual account involving that person.

A Divine Production Presents

SINCERELY HERS

A Novel

By

Shenetta Marie

DEDICATION

This one is for my family, friends, and everyone who has been supporting me on this long journey.

PROMISE

A Declaration assuring that one will or will not do something; a vow

Divine

Wonderful, perfect, beautiful, excellent, lovely, stunning, glorious, marvelous, splendid, gorgeous, delightful, exquisite, radiant, superlative, ravishing

SINCERE

Free from pretense or deceit; proceeding from genuine feelings.

(of a person) Saying what they genuinely feel or believe; not dishonest or hypocritical.

ONE

Sincere sat on Jay's couch disgusted by the sight of him. The little nigga's arrogance was off the map. He didn't mind if a nigga was feeling himself, but Jay was ridiculous with his shit. He hated the fact that Divine gave him so much leeway. If Jay was short on money it was okay, if he wasn't pushing his workers hard enough it was okay, and if he wasn't distributing the product fast enough it was okay. Any and everything that was unacceptable with someone else was acceptable when it came to her little brother. Well their little brother, but Jay didn't know that part. Once Sincere and Divine found out about their relation to one another they didn't tell anyone besides Promise, Divine's mother Victory, and Promise's mother Innocence. There wasn't any need for anyone else to know about their special bond, especially Jay.

Sincere stared at his faggot ass little brother all the while thinking there was no way in hell there was an actual cop raid. Everything about it screamed professional jack boys and he had a good idea who they could be.

❖❖❖

Promise sat inside his 2011 Chevy Suburban truck with his twenty eight month old son and his twenty five month old daughter waiting patiently for his Queen to grace them with her presence. He turned in his seat to get a good look at his children. He had fed them a healthy breakfast that morning and gave them a nice warm bath, now they sit in their car seats passed out looking like perfect angels. He stared intensively at his son. True Knowledge wasn't biologically his, but he did love him as if he created him himself.

Knowledge is the son of his childhood best friend that's now his woman, Divine. She had conceived Knowledge before they became an item. But aborting the child was never an option in Promise's eyes. He never gave her a choice.

As he gazed upon his son he could see so many features that could make the child his, but for the life of him he couldn't see any traces of his deceased biological father, Rob. Not a one. That would be something he's going to address with his Queen very soon.

He glanced over at his beautiful baby girl Treasure. He couldn't believe that such a perfect creation could come from such a corrupt person. Unlike his son his daughter was conceived when him and Divine were an item but he had no knowledge of the child's existence. One day out of the blue the mother Carmen showed up on his trap house door steps with the beautiful baby, but it's sad to say that she didn't leave with the bundle of joy. She didn't even leave with her own life, Promise made sure of that. But just like he accepted and loved her son, Divine did the same with his daughter. He jumped every hurdle to make his daughter legally Divine's.

Nothing or no one would ever break up his happy home. In his heart there wasn't an obstacle that they couldn't conquer as long as they were together.

Promise smiled at his children one last time before turning his attention to the front door of his home. As he looked down at his watch he heard the door shut. He looked up at his Queen as she locked the door then sighed *about time*.

Divine hopped in the truck closing the oversized door behind her. She glanced at her babies in the back seat then turned her attention to Promise telling him, "Let's ride."

After dropping their children off at Promise's mother's house, the two rode down Kinsman on their way to Divine's little brother's spot with no emotion on either of their faces nor in their hearts. Especially Divine, when it came to her money she had no understanding. And from what Promise had told her about the cop raid having no arrest and with them only taking the dope and the money she knew it was some bullshit in the game. Now she just hoped her brother wasn't a part of it. Yes she knew some jack boys could have pulled the move but from what she was told about the raid it sounded like it was a possible inside job. The location of the money was impossible for anyone to have stumbled across, even the police.

Divine waltzed inside Jay's spot looking as if she was ready to tangle with the devil himself. The entire world knew not to fuck with her family or her money, yet some fool played their hand anyway. She surveyed the surroundings of the living room then landing her eyes on Jay. Something about his facial expression was making her see red. She knew that dumb look from anywhere, it was the same look he had when they were growing up whenever he was caught doing something wrong. She knew the moment she started questioning him he was going to start with that stuttering shit just like their father.

She slowly walked towards her little brother stopping directly in front of him, toe to motherfucking toe. Jay tried to stand but wasn't shit happening. She pushed him right back down in his seat.

"What the fuck Sis?" Jay asked looking confused.

Divine of course gave her evil smirk then slapped him across his face with her baby nine. Blood flew out of his mouth as his face whipped to the side. She grabbed him by the chin turning his face back towards her. "I want my money and my dope. I'm going to give you 48 hours and not a minute more. I want my shit Jay!"

Sincere chuckled as he walked over to Promise, "I guess I'm not the only one that saw this fuckin' snake in the grass."

Promise held out his hand so Sincere can give him some dap responding, "Right."

Jay looked at the two men then at his big sister, "You mean to tell me you're going to let these niggas pump your head up sis? So it's going to be their word against mine? I'm your flesh and blood. These niggas ain't shit to you for real. Didn't daddy teach us that blood was thicker than water?"

Divine smiled at his statement. "Yes brother you are my flesh and blood but in this game that same flesh and blood can be this bitch down fall. And yes yo' daddy taught us that blood was thicker than water and we needed blood to live, but what he failed to tell us was that the body also needed water to survive." She pointed to Sincere and Promise, "And these two niggas right here is the water that keeps me surviving. So sorry to say little brother but yes I would take their word over yours. Hell I'll take their word over my mama's in some cases."

Turning and walking away from Jay, she stated over her shoulder, "We can stop with all the soap opera bullshit, all I want is my dope and money, and I pray you will be able to present them to me in 48 mutherfuckin' hours".

She turned to Sincere, "Don't shit move on Cedar 'til I get my shit. Not an ounce, not a gram, and damn sure not a dime bag. Sin this is for you to handle, you and you alone and I mean that shit. Do you understand me?"

"Yeah I got you Doll." Sincere answered with his usual smirk on his face as he stared at Jay.

But the order that left Sincere with a smirk on his face led to Promise having a scowl across his. "What the fuck you mean him and him alone?"

She looked at Promise sideways, "I mean exactly what the fuck I said. Now let's go."

Divine couldn't get in the car nevertheless put her seatbelt on good enough before Promise started screaming at her.

"So why the fuck you got Sin flying solo on this? It is my money and product too, so what the fuck makes you think I'm going to sit on my fuckin' hands?"

She glanced over at the love of her life. "Well number one, technically it's not your money nor is it your product and number two I don't want you handling my little brother," with her facial expression saying fuck with me if you want to.

Promise didn't hear shit she had said about him not handling her little brother, his brain was still stuck on it's not your money or your dope. Instead of even asking what the hell she was talking about he decided to keep that information to himself along with the feelings he had about his son and do some investigating of his own. Now all that was pondering in his mind was *what the fuck has his Queen been up to?*

The moment Divine walked out of the door Jay rushed to the bathroom so he could get a good look at his face. He stared at his reflection in the mirror thankful that his sister didn't fuck his shit up. What he didn't know was that his sister was seasoned when it came to pistol whippin' niggas and she knew exactly how much power to put in the blow so that she wouldn't inflict too much pain or damage upon him.

As he stared at himself in the mirror Sincere's reflection came into view. For some reason when Sincere stood behind him an eerie feeling passed over him. Actually he always got that feeling whenever Sincere was around.

"You got something you want to say?" Jay asked while putting as much bass in his voice as he could.

"That's what I should be asking you young one and I would like an answer ASAP." Sincere responded with that same disgusted look plastered on his face.

Jay matched his stare and for some reason as he truly looked at Sincere he could see something faintly familiar in his eyes, "Actually I ain't got shit to say to you, so could you please step the fuck back. This bathroom is to fuckin' small for two big niggas to be occupying its space."

Jay irked the hell out of Sincere. He couldn't understand why he couldn't stand his own brother. He and Divine always had some kind of sibling spiritual connection, but he didn't feel shit for Jay. He couldn't exactly put his finger on it but it was something about the young nigga he couldn't stand. He gave a slight smile to his little brother thinking to himself *you're more of a female than our sister*.

Jay hated when Sincere put that stupid smile on his face. "What the fuck is so funny?" He asked smirking at him through the mirror.

Sincere grabbed him by his neck so fast then started choking him responding, "As a matter of fact ain't shit funny about a hundred stacks and ten bricks of heroin. Now what you need to do is stop looking in this fuckin' mirror nursing a bloody mouth and get our shit."

He untangled his long fingers from around Jay's neck and walked out of the bathroom yelling "ASAP" over his shoulder on his way out of the front door.

TWO

Cherokee buzzed around Sincere's kitchen preparing him some dinner. The night before he seemed to be stressed so she figured she would brighten his mood with his favorite meal. He loved Olive Garden and since she loved to cook she always experimented with their recipes at home. That night she was creating the Tour of Italy meal which consisted of homemade lasagna lightly breaded chicken parmigiana and creamy fettuccine alfredo. She knew that would put a smile on her grumpy man's face.

She loved everything about Sincere, from his long sexy bow legs, his smooth dark chocolate skin, his six feet four inch height that complemented his now 210lb frame, his beautiful smile, all the way to his huge dick. The way he makes her body feel sexually was phenomenal. She had many lovers but none made her feel like her Cere did. As she set the dinner table she thought of their first encounter.

She stood in line at Two Cousins Beauty Store on 140th and Kinsman waiting patiently to pay for her items. All she had was ten packs of barrettes for her daughter Shereé but the young girl in front of her was being so indecisive about some blond weave that her dark skin tone didn't need anyway. As she stood in line shuffling her feet from side to side the smell of cologne invaded her senses. She knew the fragrance very well because it belonged to the tall sexy chocolate guy that comes into the bank where she works every Friday. It was something about the guy. The way he kept his dark piercing eyes on her while she took care of his banking transaction drove her insane.

Then when he flashed her that beautiful smile with those perfect set of white teeth telling her "thank you Ms. Kee, have a wonderful day", she instantly creamed her panties. She really loved the fact that he had given her a nickname.

When it was finally her turn to purchase her items she sighed thanking God to herself as she placed the barrettes on the counter. After hearing the total of her order she looked down in her purse to fetch the cash and then she heard that beautiful deep raspy voice saying "I got you Ms. Kee". Of course the moment she heard his voice she creamed her panties. She couldn't believe that just the sound of his voice did that to her.

Once he paid the cashier the $10.75, he grabbed the bag of barrettes then placed his hand on the small of her back ushering her out of the store. Outside of the store he walked her to her car where he hugged her around her waist pulling her close to him.

"So when are we going to stop being about business and make this thing we have more personal?" Sincere asked as he gazed into her eyes.

Smiling from ear to ear, "I don't know what thing you're referring to."

"I'm referring to this strong attraction we have for one another. And don't you dare try to deny it. You know you feel it just as much as I do. Because if you didn't you wouldn't put on that sly sexy smile when I walk into the bank and your body wouldn't shiver as you cream your panties when I tell you to have a good day."

She blushed at his comment, "What makes you think I cream my panties?"

Pulling her body into his tighter he whispered in her ear, "Because you do, just like I know they're soaking wet right now. So like I stated earlier let's stop playing banking and start playing house."

He released her from his strong embrace then guided his hand to hers retrieving her phone. Holding her cell phone in his hand he politely dialed his number so her number would appear in his phone. Once he was done he placed her phone back in her hand, gave her a gentle kiss on the cheek, walked away from her, and then jumped in his cherry red Dodge Challenger.

She couldn't believe that had happened to her. Yes she was attracted to everything about him. Yes she creamed her panties whenever he told her to have a good day, and hell yes she was soaking wet at that moment. But she has never met a man with such forwardness and aggression in her life. It somewhat frightened her but at the same damn time turned her on. Now she couldn't wait for his phone call. As she jumped in her car she had an epiphany, giving herself a sly smile she pressed the call button on her phone.

"What's good Ms. Kee?"

"What's your favorite food?"

"Um let's see, I really dig Italian food. Why?"

"Because I'm cooking you dinner tonight, it should be ready about eight. Is that a good time for you?"

"Yeah that's cool, just text me your address and I'll be there at eight sharp."

"Will do"

From that night on couldn't anyone or anything keep the two apart.

Cherokee snapped out of her flashback smiling because now here she stood in his kitchen cooking him the same exact meal that she had cooked for him the first day he had graced her small apartment with his presence. Damn she loved her man.

Sincere walked into his home with a sickening feeling plastered across his face. He was so upset that he walked right past his woman without saying a word to her and never noticing the beautiful black teddy that she was wearing while holding a silver plate filled with chocolate covered strawberries in one hand and a glass of bubbly Moscoto in the other. He marched to his man cave slamming and locking the door behind him.

Cherokee stood in her original position not understanding what happened. But what she did understand was by no means was she to dare disturb him while he was in his secluded room. That room was off limits to her. Always have been and always will be.

Instead of lingering on the situation she politely went to the kitchen fixed him a plate of food then placed it in the microwave. She cleaned up the rest of the kitchen then went upstairs to lay in their king size bed alone. Seeing as though something like this has never transpired between them she figured that's all she could do.

At 5am on the dot she heard his deep voice whisper in her ear, "Thanks for the food Kee Baby". Then she felt his hand slide down her body to her sticky core where it stayed as he fell asleep slightly snoring in her ear.

Why she wanted to shed a tear she didn't know. Maybe it was because in her heart she knew this wasn't going to be the last of some unappreciative nights.

THREE

Jay had let 18 of the 48 hours his sister had given him past by without getting anything accomplished. He had wrecked his brain over and over again trying to figure out who had robbed his spot. He knew to his sister and her pit bulls that it seemed as if he wasn't fazed or cared about what had happened but that was the furthest thing from the truth. He couldn't help that he didn't wear his anger on his sleeve and lose control when something went wrong like his sister did. The way she reacted really didn't surprise him because he knew that's who she was. But that nigga Sincere, he couldn't wait to get his revenge on him. Once he straightened this mess out with his big sis, he vowed to himself that he was going to have Sincere's head on a silver platter. But before any of that could happen he needed to talk to someone that knew the streets and the game like the back of their hand, his father.

He sighed as he sat down on his beige Italian leather sofa. He was debating if he really wanted to discuss this matter with his dad because his father was very adamant when he told him that the streets weren't for him. His dad didn't want him in the drug game by any shape, form, or fashion. If he did he would have went to his dad instead of going to Tone when he wanted to get his toes wet in the game.

He dialed his father's number and to his surprise he received the voicemail. He turned too looked at his cell with a confused look on his face. As long as he could remember he has never received his father's voicemail when he called his phone. He dialed the number numerous of times to only receive the voicemail over and over. Now realizing that it kept picking up on the first ring let him know that his father had the phone powered off. This was odd to him because he knew his father would never turn his phone off just in case of an emergency. That was a cardinal rule in their family. Phones stay on at all times. When he couldn't get in contact with his father he decided to call his sister. Even though he knew she was mad as hell about what had happened, he knew he could rely on her to help find the niggas that ran in his spot.

As Divine drove down Euclid Ave headed towards East Cleveland she started to think of her little brother. She always felt her father treated Jay better than any of his other children. Couldn't any harm come to Lil JD. Her father had twenty children, nine boys and eleven girls, but it seemed the only one that got the golden child treatment was Jason Dawson Jr.

When they moved to Shaker Heights she was able to go back down the way to kick it but not Jay, he was only allowed to play in Shaker with his suburban friends. But to her the one thing her father didn't understand was that hustling and the streets was a part of them. It flowed through their veins along with their blood. The more her father tried to shelter Jay from the streets, the more the streets called his name. That's why she didn't have any problems accepting him with open arms. But she also knew she put a lot of pressure on him making him responsible for the entire Cedar operation, but how else was he going to learn. She was a leader, Sincere was a leader even their bitch ass father was a leader, so why would she allow her little brother to be anything less. She didn't care who had anything to say about it, if they had a problem with it they would just have to see her. In her eyes no one was perfect. Everyone had to bump their head a couple of times before they got it right. So this thing with Jay getting robbed blind was one of the times she felt he bumped his head. She had a gut feeling that Jay didn't have anything to do with the fake raid, but she also knew she had to put some fire under his ass so he could be the one to figure out who did. The baby tap she gave him with her pistol wasn't enough to leave a real war wound but just enough to get him moving.

Just as she was about to bend the corner of Strathmore and Euclid her cell phone started to ring. She looked at the screen before answering then smiled to herself once she saw who was calling.

"What's good little brother? You got some good news for me?"

"I wouldn't say good news but I would like to pick your brain on this one thing."

"Yep, meet me in front of my grandmother's house in about two hours."

She hung up the phone excited that her brother made the correct decision, which was calling her.

Divine pulled up to her nigga Jamal's house to talk a little business with him but mostly so she could see his face and enjoy his company. Jamal had to be one of the funniest niggas she knew. Literally! Everything that came out his mouth was hilarious. But most of all he had one of the kindest souls she has ever known. True he was a street nigga, true he had bodied his fair share of street niggas, but all in all his heart was kind. Especially towards her!

When she ran away from her father's house after his betrayal she moved in with her mother who at the time had a small apartment in East Cleveland, Ohio. That's where she first met Jamal when she had started attending Shaw High School in her tenth grade year. They actually shared a biology class together. But on her first day at the new school when Jamal entered the classroom she couldn't stand the sight of him. He was the biggest bully she had ever come in contact with. Really! He picked on every male in the class. And it seemed he had already had a reputation going for himself because everyone seemed to be scared of him, even the damn teacher because he never asked the disruptive Jamal to leave the classroom. But by the second week of school she realized he wasn't so much of a bully, just a class clown. He even had her laughing at his retarded ass jokes.

By her third week at the school her friend Samantha told her that Jamal didn't act like that all the time and that he was just showing out for her. She didn't believe that to be true but sure enough by the time the snow hit the ground Jamal had asked her to be his girl.

She had never had a boyfriend and really wasn't planning on having one. Jamal would be the first but she told herself what the hell they were all the way out in East Cleveland who was going to find out. She kicked it in EC all through the school week and made her way down the way or either to Kinsman County on the weekends.

She really liked Jamal because he was kind of a square kid, nothing like what she was raised around. He didn't sell drugs. He worked at the East Side Market. He didn't shoot niggas for recreation. He trained as a boxer at the East Cleveland PAL gym. He wasn't trying to fuck every girl that walked past him. He was actually still a virgin at the tender age of sixteen. But once he hooked up with her all the good boy act went straight out of the window.

See from the moment Jamal noticed Divine in his biology class he had already known who she was. He remembered seeing her a few years back on Northfield getting in and out of a beige 300E Mercedes Benz. He thought she was the most beautiful girl he has ever seen and he also knew if given the opportunity he would have to step his game up because he could tell she came from money. So once Divine obliged him by being his girl he quickly adopted the streets for his source of income, quitting the East Side Market. He stopped going to the gym as hugging the block became his new recreation. And he also lost his virginity to the female he had been crushing on since he had seen her on Northfield some years back. From the very first day Divine gave him a chance their relationship blossomed as well did a beautiful friendship. Monday through Friday the two were inseparable during their high school years.

Promise sat in one of his jump offs car in Family Dollar parking lot staring intensively across the street at Divine politicking with some big black EC nigga. She was sitting on the nigga porch chopping it up with him like she has known him her entire life. And that couldn't be possible because if she had known him for that long then so should he. He couldn't believe how she was sitting on the porch cracking up at the nigga like he was the funniest man on earth. As long as he had known her he has never seen her so giddy around anyone. Her demeanor was usually the more serious type. Even if someone did or said some funny shit she would just give a slight chuckle.

"Okay Mal enough with the jokes and shit with your crazy ass, how many of them chickens are you going to need this trip?"

Ready to discuss business himself Jamal put his serious face on. "You right Vines joke time is over, but um I think we can rock wit 'bout two of 'em this week. It's light weight a drought out this way so I should be able to rock those real quick."

Divine sat in deep thought, if it was a drought and if Mal will probably be the only one with some quality coke shit she was thinking she should drop four of them things in his lap.

"If it's a shortage why do you only want to rock with two? That's only going too lead to me coming right back out here within a day or two because you're going to be calling me for two more."

Sitting on the porch banister Jamal gave her a sly sexy smile, "Maybe that's what I want. Maybe I want you back out my way in another day or two. You know you've been missing in action for damn near a year now."

"Well if that's what you want all you have to do is call me and say that then. There's no need for me to be riding out this way like UGK twice in one week. I'll bring what you need in one whop and then if you want to see me you know I'm always one phone call away Mal," she said returning the sly sexy smile.

"That's what's up Vines, if that's the case gone and bring four my way and I'll make sure I call so I can get some time in with you."

As she stood giving Jamal a hug she noticed the 2012 Silver Honda Accord sitting across the street in Family Dollar parking lot. She actually noticed it following her throughout the day. She smiled saying to herself *I see you Promise and you got the nerve to be following me around in your bitch car, shame on you Don.*

FOUR

Sincere had finally caught up with his cousin Diamond. Her ass had been MIA every since he had put her on to Detective Barns some months back. Yeah she has been checking in with the Fam but not like she should have. He was starting to believe that she was taking the job he gave her a little too far. The only thing he required her to do was to get close to the detective to see if they were up to something when he and Promise seen the two detectives on Cedar, not for her to make a happy home with the damn police.

He watched as she got out of a Taurus SEL looking fly as hell. True she was always dressed nice but it was that around the way fly girl look. Today she looked as if she was on another level with her shit getting her grown woman on. She rocked a black Silk Chiffon Blouse with some black Double Knit Ponte Leggings with some Patchwork Ballet Flats. She had copped the entire outfit from Brook Brothers a store she thought only white girls shopped at but now she sees that they have some fly things in there. It was safe to say that Brook Brothers was now her favorite store.

"What's up cousin?" Diamond asked as she slid her slender frame into the passenger seat of his car.

"Shit! That's what I should be asking you," Sincere responded as he looked her over checking out her new style. "I see you got your big girl shit on. When did you get a makeover?"

Now giving herself a once over, "I know I'm looking good right. John thought I should step my game up a little so he helped me get on my grown woman shit in the attire category."

He looked at her crazy and hoped when he asked her his next question that she didn't give him a retarded answer. "Who the fuck is John?"

"Barns, crazy."

Looking at her as if she has lost her mind he asked, "You mean Detective Barns as in the police?"

"Yes him Sincere."

"You're talking about him like he your man or something."

"I mean we cool, he's not that bad Sin. And he takes care of me very swell so that's even more of a plus."

"Cousin I'm cool wit' the nigga taking care of you that was kind of the purpose. We needed you to get close to him and have him comfortable enough to tell you his business. But so far you haven't reported shit back to us. Like you don't know what team you're playing for?"

"Don't mistake it Sin, I know my place. But I'm just saying he's not all that bad and I have taken a liking towards him and as long as he's not aiming at my families head then everything is cool. But all in all you're right so let me give you the updates. No he's not a dirty cop. He says he's on a special task force unit where they shut down upcoming drug operations and in return they get big bonuses and incentives. He did tell me that Kinsman County is off limits to their force though."

"You mean to tell me that you told him about our family?"

"No I did not Sincere. I'm not fucking stupid and I'm tired of you trying to play me like I am. He was just talking about what he do and how it was one neighborhood on their list that was untouchable and that he didn't have any clue as to why. When I asked him what hood it was he told me the upper part of Kinsman."

"Well let me ask you this, did his team get a big bonus lately?"

"Yeah he told me they raided some up and coming lil nigga's spot on Buckeye. He said for the nigga to be just starting out he was sitting on a whole lot of money and dope."

"What kind of dope?"

"He said the young dude had like ten keys of heroin."

"Now cousin I want you to really think about this. We're in the heroin game and heavy at that, what nigga do you know on Buckeye getting money like that especially wit' that dog food? Buckeye is known to have that white girl all day every day, not that boy. So do you think he might have lied to you about their last bust?"

"He could have, but why?"

Yeah why, Was exactly what Sincere was thinking to himself?

Sincere left Diamond with one thing on his mind. There was no way they got ten keys of dog food off any nigga on Buckeye and it damn sure wasn't a coincidence that, that was the exact amount that came up missing out of Jay's spot.

Divine pulled up in front of her Grandmother's house thirty minutes early so she could kick it with her favorite lady for a couple of minutes before her brother got there but to her surprise Jay was already there posted in his car.

She approached the passenger side of his car poking her head through the window. "Give me 'bout two minutes Brother let me go holla at my grandma real quick."

The moment she sat her backside in the passenger seat of Jay's car he started pleading his case.

"Sis I have dismantled my brain on this shit and I know it may look a little out of place seeing as though there weren't any arrest. But I promise you the muthafuckas that came up in my spot was the police. Rather they're legit police that I don't know but police is what they were Sis.

She sat with her head resting on the head rest of the seat thinking. She tilted her head up and down real slow as she played with her bottom lip. A habit that she didn't know she had until Promise had pointed it out to her.

"Sooooo that's your story and your sticking to it?" She asked as she tilted her head to the side staring at her little brother out the corner of her eye.

Jay sat with his head down staring into his lap clenching his hands together. "Man Sis, I'm telling you how all that shit went down, them niggas movement, and the orders they were throwing around was like some military shit. I got my little niggas on it seeing if they or anyone else had seen some suspicious cars hanging around our way in the past couple of months because whoever came up in my spot did their homework. So I'm on it, I don't want you to think I'm bullshitting around you know cause that deadline you got me on coming up real soon."

"I got you Brother, as of now your deadline is extended 'til we get this shit settled. You don't have to worry about your big sister going loco on you anymore."

"I'm glad you brought that up because on the real Sis that nigga Sincere is all out of pocket. I'm not going to involve you but just so you know that nigga is on my shit list. Really!"

Divine look at her little brother proudly and crazy at the same time, proud because she could see some gangster in him but crazy because there was no way he was going to do a damn thing to Sincere. "What the hell you mean by he's on your shit list."

Jay cocked his head to the side and turned his face up to her, "Exactly what the fuck I said."

"Okay well I guess what I'm asking is what the hell being on your shit list mean? You trying to do some bodily harm to the man or what?"

"That's not your concern Sis, this between two grown ass men."

She laughed at the comment, "Correct me if I'm wrong but ain't you only eighteen? What in the world is grown about that?"

"I do grown man shit so that makes me grown."

"Okay I got you little brother. Gone wit' yo' grown self."

She did a head to toe on her brother and she has to say that he is forming into 'That Nigga'!

Jay stood at five feet ten inches with bow legs with slightly slew feet. His mocha brown complexion felt baby soft, and his dreamy bedroom eyes drove the young girls' bananas along with his smooth soft voice. But what was most handsome about him was his charisma. He has a caring personality and keeps himself very well groomed. True Jay drove the young girls insane but his pleasure was older females. He preferred his women to be at least five years his senior. If she had to categorize him he would fit along the lines of the metrosexual type. A well-groomed man with lots of money who loves to shop and get pampered living in an urban community. That was her brother all day. Now as she sat observing him she could see that gangster part of him as well.

Divine smiled to herself admiring how her brother was coming into his own.

As soon as she departed from her brother Sincere started ringing her cell.

"What's good Twin?"

"We need to talk, now!"

"Yep, where do you want me to meet you at?"

"On my way to Whitmores, so head up there." Sincere stated then hanging up his phone.

Divine walked up to Sincere and gave him a bear hug from behind. She then gave him a peck on the cheek and asked, "What's up Twin?"

"Some serious shit, that's what."

She took his statement as a queue to sit down on the bar stool beside him. She then signaled the bartender to bring her normal shot of Remy Martin VSOP. "Shoot Sin!"

He inhaled deeply, "Long story short, I caught up with your sister-in-law to get some updates on Barns. When she got out of her car she was looking fly ass shit which is cool but when I asked what the change was all about she tells me that John said she needs to step her game up".

"Who the fuck is John?" She asked with her face turned up.

"That's exactly what I said. And guess who the nigga is, none other than Detective Barns."

"What? She's talking about him on a first name basis with you?'

Sincere threw his hands up, "Right! I knew I wasn't going to be the only one to see something wrong with that. But anyway she goes on to tell me that he's not a crooked cop like we thought but he is part of some special task force that close up upcoming niggas shops, says the bigger the bust the bigger the bonus. So then I ask did they come into a real big bust lately and this broad tells me that they ran up in some nigga on Buckeye spot getting ten bricks of dog food, but he didn't tell her how much cash they got."

The very instant 'ten bricks' left his mouth Divine was on it. "What muthafuckin' nigga on Buckeye got dog food like that? Man Sin that shit just ain't no coincidence. Please don't tell me she's that fuckin' naïve?"

"Either that Twin or her ass had in on it, like we said the place the cash was hidden at them muthafuckas shouldn't have stumbled across it."

She rubbed her hands down her face. "I just left from talking with Jay and he is very adamant about them being the police that ran up in there. He said that shit was too organized."

"Well maybe the lil bro right on this one Doll. Damn!"

She turned to give Sincere a confused look. "Why you say damn like that?"

"It ain't shit." He responded as he thought of how he choked his brother out.

FIVE

Promise hasn't been home in a couple of days but Divine wasn't going to let that bother her. She was so over him getting in his feelings and disappearing when something wasn't going his way. She saw the nigga clear as day when she was over Jamal's house and the nigga had the audacity to be in that hoe Trish car. Like really. She thought he was so funny with him thinking he knew every move that she made. Only if he really knew the half of what she was about. But she on the other hand knew every move he made, even before he made it. He was so loose with his shit at times. Maybe that was because she always turned the other cheek to his indiscretions. If his other women were helping to put food on the Fams table then his sluts got a pass. But this shit he was doing with his new female Trish couldn't buy her a pair of Christian Louboutin pumps, which meant her Don had been fucking for pleasure and not for business. Now that was some unacceptable shit in her eyes.

With all that being said she decided to say fuck Promise and focus on her children for the rest of day. She figured they were long overdue for a Chuck E Cheese visit so that's where she would be spending the rest of her evening, with her babies.

Promise returned to his spacious South Woodland home at four in the morning feeling depleted. For the life of him he couldn't put his finger on his Queens latest actions. The first thing he did when he entered his home was take a hot relaxing shower because if he didn't he probably would have went straight to his bedroom and strangled Divine to death in their king sized bed.

After his shower he peeked in on his sleeping angels. It cracked him up how the two couldn't sleep apart. Even though they had their own beds they slept in one bed together every night. Be it Knowledge's or Treasure's room it didn't matter as long as they were together. When he was done checking on his babies he made his way to the master bedroom and said a silent prayer before entering. Once inside he slid in bed behind the woman he would kill for, hell the woman he has killed for. The moment his body touched the mattress Divine automatically positioned herself in her usual place, snuggled closed to him with her face pressed in his chest. Instantly he forgot all about her new actions that had his mind going insane and wanted nothing more but to be inside of her. It seemed as if he hasn't felt his heaven's walls in an eternity.

Before she could inhale his scent well she felt his head between her legs earning his lickin' license as always. From the moment he spread her pussy lips taking that first sinful lick her eyes rolled to the back of her head as she gripped his head letting him know she wanted more. When a nigga ate pussy as good as Promise did how the hell could she ever stay mad at him was beyond her. And as well as he ate pussy she knew hers was the only one he was blessing with that good head of his. She didn't care how many other women he had she knew all they were getting was the dick and if they we're happy with just dick then so was she.

Between licks he began to speak, "You're starting to underestimate me Doll, that's not a good thing to do."

With a loud moan she told him, "Me underestimate you, never. I know what I'm dealing with."

"You sure about that?" He asked then dug his face into her pussy sucking on her clit as if his life depended on it.

She couldn't keep her composure, "Oh my Goddddd, yessssss Don I'm sure."

"I'm just making sure you know."

After that there were no more words to be said. Only thing could be heard was him licking at his heaven and with her screaming for the good Lord once her cum slid down Promise's throat.

He looked up at his Queen from between her healthy thighs thinking how much he loved his woman and vowed to himself once again there wasn't anything going to stand in the way of their love. If she was making money moves outside of him that was cool. Hell he made money moves outside of her so why should he bitch about her being about a dollar. As long as his home life was good then so was he.

The next morning Divine woke up to the smell of turkey sausage, cheese eggs, grits, and Grands butter biscuits. She got out of bed then headed to Treasure's room since that's the room the children decided to sleep in last night. She opened up the door slowly only to see her daughter wide awake but knew she wasn't going to move from her spot until her brother was awake also.

"Gone head and wake him up Baby Girl."

On cue Treasure started tapping on Knowledge telling him to wake up. After they both was wide awake she took them to the bathroom to give them their morning wash up.

She and the children finally made it to the kitchen where Promise was waiting patiently at the table with all their plates made.

"Don't think I didn't see you stalking me the other day." She stated after taking her first bite of food.

"I know you saw me. I wasn't hiding!" He responded with his face saying (and).

"So do you want to tell me who ole boy is and what you were doing with him?"

"He's my EC nigga and we were handling business."

Giving her that slanted look with his sexy brown eyes he asked "What kind of business?"

"White boy business"

Now giving her a confused look, "When did you get into the white boy business?"

"About three years ago." She responded as she shrugged her shoulders like that wasn't anything major.

"Why didn't I know anything about that?"

"Well at the time it wasn't anything for you to know. It was something I started myself on that side of town. But since you're back in your stalking mode I just

wanted to let you know what was going on before you start getting the wrong ideas."

Shaking his head, "You have no idea about the wrong ideas I got going through my mind right about now. But now isn't the time to discuss it. We shouldn't be discussing anything right now anyway it's my babies' time."

With that being said he turned his attention to his children telling himself he would deal with her at a later time.

After breakfast Divine decided she would spend the rest of the day in the house spending time with Knowledge and Treasure. If it was one thing she was tired of about the streets was that they were stealing time from her family.

SIX

Cherokee dressed slowly thinking of her and Sincere. They had been so distant that it has been affecting her spirit. She barely wanted to go to work at times, whatever energy she did have she had been using it on her daughter. As she dressed for work she realized that she hasn't been to the spa in a while. "It is definitely time for another visit" She spoke as she picked up her phone deciding to call Divine.

"What's good Kee?"

"Girl nothing much, but my mind has been all over the place so I'm in desperate need of a spa day."

"I feel you on that, gone and make us a reservation and let me know. I got the ticket too this time."

"Okay I'll let you know when."

"Yup" Divine responded thankful for the invite. She loved spa days with Cherokee but between her kids, her dope business, and her Promise she rarely got a chance to go anymore.

After speaking with her good friend, Cherokee felt a little more at ease. Now with some pep in her step she dressed for work. Being the sophisticated girl that she was she threw on her black and white Annabelle sleeveless lace top with her Sabrina sequined skirt, some sheer black stockings with her black peep-toe platform pumps by Guess then grabbed her daughter and headed out the door for work.

Jay decided to make this beautiful Wednesday morning be the day he decides to go to Key Bank and open up a savings account. He reasoned with himself that all his drug money didn't belong at home in a safe where some jack boys could get their hands on it. Some of the money belonged in the bank accruing some interest for a rainy day. If the bank got robbed it was cool because all of the money is insured so he knew his funds would be safe there.

Cherokee smiled at the male version of Divine as he entered the bank. She waved him over to her.

"What's good Cherokee? I didn't know you worked here."

Giving him a sheepish smile, "Yes this would be me. Now what can I do for you today?"

"I wanted to open up a savings account."

"Well the only way I can help you with that is to direct you to our accounts manager. That's where you open new accounts."

"Okay thanks. But what time is your lunch break? Maybe we can go grab something to eat."

"Awww, thanks for the offer Jay but Sincere is coming to pick me up for lunch today."

"That's cool, well maybe another day then." Jay told her as he slid his number across the counter.

She sat smiling at the number looking like a school girl with a high school crush. Young Jay wanted to take her out to lunch, how cute was that. She admired his sexy legs as he walked over to the accounts manager desk. *Yes maybe another day.*

Sincere got tired of Cherokee calling his phone so he decided to turn it off. He knew he told her that he was picking her up for lunch but some business came up. Yes he could have texted her to let her know that something came up but texting wasn't his thing, it was hers. So he said fuck it he would make it up to her later.

"So Fox you telling me this nigga legit, a nigga from the Wood wanting that much dog food is unusual. Are you positive he not the police?"

"Sin I'm positive man. He's from Longwood but that's not where he kick it at. He moved from down here to Superior when we was about sixteen. His grandmother still stays down here so he slides through a lot."

"Alright my nigga, long as you know you're the one vouching for the nigga."

"I got you Sin."

Cherokee stood at the rear entrance of Key Bank tapping her foot rapidly as she waited for Sincere to pull up. He was only running about five minutes late but that had her heated. For her he was usually sitting in the parking lot about ten minutes early, so it was safe to say she was in her feelings. Even more so after standing there for thirty minutes and he still haven't arrived nor has he been answering his phone. Before she knew it her one hour lunch break was over and she still hadn't eaten. She was now beyond heated as she walked back to her work station behind the counter hungry as hell. Four o'clock couldn't come fast enough.

⁂

Quan had been making a lot of money with that white boy on Superior and with the prices his nigga Legend was setting them birds out for he was eating very well. But fucking with his uncle he now sees a demand for heroin in his neighborhood. And what was crazy was that it wasn't the old school niggas that wanted it, it was the young dudes.

One day when he went behind the BP gas station on the corner of Superior and Parkwood to take a piss to his surprise it was a dude all of fifteen years old nodded out with a needle sticking out of his arm. He couldn't believe what he was seeing and he has seen some crazy shit in his life. But from seeing the young dude and with his uncle knowing a lot of cats that used then he knew he was making dog food his next move. He wanted to make money from every angle. He was starting to think he should fuck with some pills too. The females loved that ecstasy shit.

Sincere watched the Superior nigga for about thirty minutes from across the street before deciding to call him to let him know he was in the area. He wanted to see what kind of niggas he was cliqued with and how he carried himself. He wasn't trying to do business with any young wild dudes. From what he saw the young one's swag seemed to be plain and business like. He wasn't wearing his pants hanging off his butt and he wasn't wearing loud flashy jewelry like the others around him. He also wasn't loud talking and cracking jokes like them either. He was pulling niggas to the side having private one on one conversations. From what he could see from afar he liked what he saw. Doing business with the young one might be good for him. He shared the profits of Kinsman County with Divine and Promise, Divine had Cedar and now he was going to have Superior.

"Your dude seems to be about his business." Sincere exclaimed to Fox.

"That's what I tried to tell you in the beginning. He used to be flashy but he told me that his dude Legend told him being flashy would bring too much attention to himself so he said he toned it down. He's been on his boss shit every since."

"Legend" Sincere said out loud with a confused look on his face. "Legend I think I heard of him before."

"I'm pretty sure you have, he's on the level of cocaine like you are with that boy. So he be gettin' that bread."

"That's what's up. I might have to hook up with him one day when I'm ready to get my feet wet with that coke shit. But let me call your boy so I can get this shit over wit'. I'm trying to see some big booty hoes shake their asses tonight."

Fox held out his hand for some dap, "Now that's what the fuck I'm talking about, Tops and mutherfuckin' Bottoms!"

"What's good Quan?" Sincere asked as he looked at Quan step away from the group to answer his phone.

Looking at his watch Quan replied, "Shit, waiting on you so I can hurry up and slide to the other side of town".

"Well I'm right across the street in the old school Impala."

Quan turned to his right and sure enough there sat the Impala. The nigga had been sitting on his block scoping him out the entire time. But he wasn't mad about that, at least he knows that Sincere is the type of nigga that does his homework because he didn't want to do business with no sloppy want to be businessmen.

After an intense meeting Quan put in an order for a half a brick of heroin to see how well it would move. If he could dump it within a weeks' time he was going to cop two more bricks, then they would go from there. The more he dumped the more he would cop.

Sincere had every intention of going straight home to kick it with Cherokee after his business meeting but Fox had draped him off into some other shit. After parlaying in Longwood for about four hours the two made their way down to the strip club Tops and Bottoms. The club wasn't a large establishment but was big enough where a nigga could get comfortable and have a good time.

Upon entering the club all that could be heard was Two Chains latest single Birthday Song. As the song played all Sincere could do was agree as he sang along, "All I want for my birthday is a big booty hoe" because that's exactly what he wanted for the night. Yes he loved his Cherokee and her petite frame but every now and then he loved to indulge between a pair of big juicy thighs. He loved looking at a fat ass when he was hitting it from the back enjoying the view of the wave.

As he walked up the stairs to the VIP section his favorite stripper Beauty caught his attention as she spun around the pole but that wasn't what he wanted for the night either. He wanted a small waist with fat ass booty cheeks that he could spread apart and once he reached the top of the stairs he bumped right into her. Grabbing her by her waist he put his dibs in for the night. "We're getting a room. I'll be outside waiting on you when you get off."

"Three o'clock sharp" was her only reply as she made her way down the stairs to take the stage.

Announcer: "Coming to the stage next isn't your ordinary stripper. Actually she says she's not a stripper at all but an exotic dancer. Ladies and gentlemen please put your hands together for Sensual."

Sensual stepped on the stage as Ciara's song Promise began to play. Her movement was so soft and sensual just like her name. Sincere stared in amazement as she danced around the stage. She had to be the most beautiful blackest female he had ever laid eyes on. He loved her dark skin tone. He didn't have the words for her body, saying she was built up like a stallion was an understatement. As he watched all he could think of was that she had to be a descendant of an African Queen. The entire time she danced around the stage she made sure to keep eye contact with Sincere keeping him captivated in a trance. For her final act she climbed to the top of the pole turned her body so she was upside down then she slid down the pole slowly clapping her thick booty cheeks together all the way down the pole. Everyone in the club except for Sincere erupted with applause. He was too busy holding his manhood trying to talk it down. "Down boy three o'clock will be here before we know it."

After doing a couple of hours of hot steamy sex with Sensual Sincere finally made his way home at six thirty in the morning. And even after him busing two loads off onto Sensual's ass cheeks his woman's petite frame turned him on as he stood at the bedroom door watching her sleep. Even though he had a shower back at the hotel he decided to take another one before he got in bed with his baby.

Cherokee felt Sincere's presence the moment he stepped through their bedroom door. She listened as he took a quick shower knowing in her heart that he was out fucking someone else. Their sex life had dwindled for the past couple of weeks but she wasn't really sure if it was because he was having sex with someone else or if he was stressed out. No way by far was she a dummy she knew that Sincere still had an abundance of hoes in the streets but never have their presence interrupted her sex life with her man. Now here this nigga come in at six thirty in the morning jumping in the shower. She was now getting fed up with his shit. His reasons for being so distant towards her lately had her baffled. They haven't had a fight or miscommunication or anything like that it just seemed that one day he woke up and became distant. She was now starting to wonder was he tired of her being there.

Sincere lie next to her and fell into his natural routine guiding his hand to her sticky core. Once she felt his fingers fondling her she knew he wanted sex and on this bright and early am she was not going to cooperate so she moved his hand then turned to lay on her stomach. From her actions Sincere felt a feeling he didn't realize that existed inside of him, jealousy. He hopped out of bed turned on the bedroom light made his way back to the bed turned her over and began to interrogate her.

"What the fuck you doing moving my hand?"

"I'm not in the mood Sincere."

"What the fuck you mean you're not in the mood? You fucking somebody else?"

She stared intensively at him not believing them words fell from his lips. After all the emotional stress he has been putting her through that was the first thing that came to his mind, her fucking somebody else.

"I'm not but you are so like I said I'm not in the mood."

He stared back at her knowing she wasn't fucking anyone else so he turned the light off then hopped back into bed. He had to turn her back over on her back since she decided to turn on her stomach again. He laid on top of her then buried himself deep inside of her. One thing about his boo he didn't really have to worry about too much foreplay because her pussy stayed wet. He stared down at her, "I don't care who or what I've been fucking, when I come to you all you need to do is play your fucking position."

That's exactly what she did played her position as he dug deep inside of her. She wrapped her legs around his waist digging her nails in his ass cheeks making him grind even harder.

"Damn Kee Baby, If only you knew how good this pussy feels to me."

Squeezing his ass even tighter, "It must not feel too good you can't keep your dick in your pants while you're in the streets."

He bit her shoulder blade then whispered in her ear, "What I do with my dick in the streets isn't your concern." Now cupping her ass and digging his nails in deep, "You just make sure this good pussy stay ready for me when I get home. Do you understand me?"

Pulling him deeper inside of her she moaned "Yes Sincere."

SEVEN

Promise was never the one to discuss or look for advice about Divine but now he needed some. He didn't want to talk to Sincere about her because that was his sister so he decided to go holla at Pops. He needed some old school advice. As he rode down 146th and Kinsman he could see that the business was booming as usual, all the junkies was out trying to get their daily fix.

When he pulled in front of Pops house he knew something wasn't right. As long as he has known the older cat he has never seen his front door open. His house was always closed up tight. No one from the hood has ever been inside of his spot, not even Promise and him and Pops were close. He walked up the front steps peeking inside the screen door. No motions could be seen from the outside looking in. He then started knocking on the door calling Pops name only to get no response in return. He pulled his Desert Eagle off his hip then proceeded inside the house with caution praying that nothing has happened to Pops. From what he could see upon entrance looked as if a robbery had taken place. Everything in the house was turned over. He made his way back to the living room wondering who in the hell would have the nerve to rob Pops and where the hell was Pops anyway. He couldn't remember a time of him going on the block and Pops not being around. All the shopping he did was in the neighborhood. Bottom line was Pops never ventured to far away from Kinsman.

As he started turning furniture back over putting things in place where he thought they belonged he stumbled across something very strange. There were pictures of him from different stages of his life and he could tell all the pictures were taking from a distance. None of them were pictures that he could remember posing for. Pops had pictures of him as a baby in a stroller, pictures of him playing in his front yard as a toddler, pictures of him playing on the school playground, and pictures of him on the block. He even had pictures of Innocence and his siblings. He stood in the middle of the living room scratching his head wondering what the fuck was going on. He stormed out of the house saying fuck putting things back in place but he did lock the bottom lock and close the front door. He made his way to his truck heading to his mother's house. He needed answers and he needed them as soon as possible.

When he got to his mother's house he was greeted with another surprise. His Baby Doll was sitting on the floor watching Dora the Explorer with their children. Divine turned to look at him and could instantly see that something was very wrong. Knowledge and Treasure automatically jumped up from the floor running to embrace their father so he had to suppress his feelings for the time being. He didn't want his children to sense that something was wrong with their daddy. He threw a big smile on his face picked up his babies then smothered them with kisses. Even though she wanted to defuse the situation and put the children back in front of the TV so she could see what was bothering her Don she also knew never to disturb him when he was interacting with his kids. She couldn't help but watch and admire the relationship he had with the children. Their children happiness and wellbeing came before anything else in their corrupted world. Instead of watching from the sideline she decided to join in the festivities.

After tiring out the kids Divine took the opportunity to see what was going on with her man. Sitting on his lap wrapping her arms around his neck she asked "What's going on Don?"

"Where is Innocence?" He asked noticing that she was nowhere around.

"She took Destiny to the mall. Now tell me what's going on with you."

"What makes you think something is going on?"

"Come on now baby you know I know when something is wrong with my heart so talk to me."

He smiled at her statement. Even though he felt that she was living foul behind his back he knew without a shadow of a doubt that her heart belonged to him. He went on to tell the chain of events of what happened at Pops house not even believing it as he spoke it.

"Don, wait you're telling me that Pops has pictures of you from different stages of your life and pictures of your family?"

"That's what I'm telling you."

She turned her face up, "What the fuck is that about?"

"Right!"

Divine left Promise at his mother's house with the children because he said he wasn't budging until Innocence got home so she took the opportunity to go and holla at Sincere to see if he had any answers about her money. She picked up her cell to give him a call, "What's good Twin, where you at?"

"Down in the Wood fucking wit Fox."

"Okay I'm headed down that way."

She rode down Kinsman headed towards the projects with one person on her mind, Pops. At the time when Promise was telling her she didn't want to say what she believed because she thought she was thinking way too far. Her brain worked that way sometimes. And if what she was thinking was true things can get real ugly for Pops.

By the time she made it to the projects she could understand why Sincere was down there, the jets were jumping.

Longwood projects may have been full of crime but they were also full of unity. Before any grimy shit went on between niggas they would instruct all of the young children to go home or go in anyone's home for that matter. If an adult saw a child doing something wrong they would gladly take that child home to their parent. And if someone was in need of something someone would find a way to help that person out be it food, clothes, or even a number to somewhere for assistance. And the niggas, she loved Longwood niggas. They had that New York swag.

All in all she loved the projects. She could remember a time when she and Sincere kicked down in Longwood almost every day of the week, leaving Promise on Kinsman where anyone could find him as always. She couldn't understand how he wouldn't venture out to different neighborhoods. But he sure made it a priority when he was following and stalking her.

She got out of her car saying *"Welcome to the jungle"*. Because that's exactly what Longwood was the motherfucking jungle. It buzzed with all kinds of walks of life. Crackheads, junkies, prostitutes, weed heads, X-heads, and most of all niggas and bitches. And that's what she saw niggas and bitches out kicking it having a good time.

She walked up to Sincere "Damn Sin it's jumping down here today."

"Sure is. But what got you down this way?" He replied as he embraced his little sister.

"Shit nigga you. I can't find you up in Kinsman County anymore."

"Whatever! So what's up?"

"Wanted to know if you heard anything else about that one thing?" She asked as she slid her hand in his sweatpants pocket to retrieve some gum that she knew was there.

"Well the more info I get out of Diamond the more I know for a fact that them dirty ass cops ran up in there. You can bet your last dollar on that shit. So now what we need to figure out is are we going to get your shit from the cops or are you going to take this one as a loss?"

She stared into her big brother eyes. Did she want to go up against the police or not. Were ten bricks and a hundred racks worth it? She gave him her infamous crooked smile, "Nigga we going up against the police. That's too much paper to be chalkin' as a loss."

He grabbed his little sister giving her a kiss on the forehead, "Now that's what the fuck I'm talkin' 'bout!"

The moment Innocence walked through her front door Promise was on it. He didn't even give her a chance to sit down and relax. He instructed his little sister to watch his kids then was out the door pulling his mother behind him.

"Ma how good is your memory?" He asked her as he parked his truck a couple of houses down from Pops house.

"Come on now son you know I don't forget anything."

"That's what I was banking on. I'm going to show you this guy then I want you to tell me everything you remember about him."

She looked at her oldest son confused, "You're saying that as if I know him or something."

"Maybe you do or maybe you don't but we're going to sit here until we find out." Those were the last words Promise spoke to his mother as he focused his attention on stalking Pops spot.

Pops came strolling down his street with groceries in his hands oblivious to the fact that he was being stalked and also that his house was robbed.

Promise looked over at his mother knowing that he didn't even have to ask her did she know the older light skinned man carrying the two Save a lots bags in his hands. Her facial expression gave her away. He pulled his truck away from the curb slowly heading back to his mother's house.

Pops fate was sealed from a facial expression.

EIGHT

After picking up the kids and getting them settled for the night all Divine wanted to do was ride her Don's dick. Not just for her but for him also. When she first arrived to their home all she saw was death written all over his face so that night was going to be the night that she pampered her man. Normally he would wash her but it was time for her to reverse their roles. She ran them a hot bubble bath and placed scented candles around the bathroom.

When he entered the bathroom he was mesmerized to see his Queen standing there in all her naked glory. Waving his hand in the direction of the tub he asked, "What's this all about?"

"It's all about you daddy." She replied as she approached him to undress him. As she guided his shirt over his head she took the opportunity to admire his many tattoos. She traced each one softly with her finger tips making sure she grazed his nipples as her fingers passed by them. She made her way down to his belt buckle making sure she stared in his pretty brown eyes as she unfastened it. After fully undressing him she led him to the bath tub. Inside she made sure she washed and massaged every nook and cranny of his body. She stood in front of him and washed herself when she was done with him. Before she could get a chance to wash her pussy he grabbed the soapy washcloth out of her hand.

"Baby I got it. It's all about you this time. All I want you to do is to sit back and enjoy the show."

Never entertaining her statement he proceeded to wash her pussy. When done he took the stopper out of the tub and turned on the shower water. He pushed her back against the cool shower tiles then kneeled down in front of her. He told her to open her legs so he could spread her juicy lips.

After taking one sinful lick he looked up at her, "I don't know when you're going to learn that when it comes to my heaven you have no say so."

She knew he was absolutely right, his heaven was his heaven and with that being said she tilted her head back against the shower walls enjoying the feel of her Don tantalizing her clit. And tantalize is what he done. He licked her clit ever so slightly teasing the hell out of her. He teased it until it became swollen as if it itself was begging him to make it cum. But that wasn't what he wanted as of yet so he continued to lick in slow circles around her swollen bud.

She couldn't take the drama he was putting her pussy through. "Please baby I can't take it. Suck it please."

He gave a slight chuckle loving to hear her beg. He now took the opportunity to lick the running juices off her inner thigh. That move alone sent her overboard. As a tear slid down her left cheek she pushed her pelvis forward grabbed his head forcing him to put his tongue in its proper place. "Daddy please suck it. Please!"

Even though he loved to tease her and his heaven he loved the feel of drinking her cum even more. So yeah she can be the boss this round. He gripped her clit with his lips and began to suck painfully slow. He was sucking her clit so good she felt like her legs were going to buckle beneath her. What her pussy was feeling was something she wouldn't dare attempt to explain. And then it happened, he began sucking her clit fast sending vibrations through her entire body making her cum harder than she has ever cum before. With glossed eyes she stared down at the love of her life instructing him to lie back. She mounted him loving the feel of his juicy dick inside of her. As she felt his manhood rubbing against her special spot she began to ride him very slow bringing her pussy to the tip of his dick then gliding it back down real slow. She was planning on paying him back for teasing her clit the way he did but that wasn't what her little lady wanted so she began to ride him at rapid speed.

She bounced up and down on his dick so fast that all he could do was take a hold of healthy hips and pray that she didn't make him bust in the matter of minutes. But once she started cumming with her pussy pulsating on his dick he came in the matter of seconds. After making him cum she hopped off his dick then buried it deep in her mouth getting it back hard instantly.

"I want to know what it feels like to swallow Don. You think we can make that happen tonight?"

"Cut the shower off and go get in the bed then you can swallow all you want."

The moment his back touched the bed she had him back in her mouth. She placed soft kisses around the head of his dick then kissing down one side of his shaft then up the other. When she reached the top she opened wide and slid her mouth down his thick pole 'til it reached the back of her throat.

He gripped her hair once she made it back to the top and began sucking only the tip. "Damn Doll, just like that baby."

His words of encouragement had her bobbing her head tantalizing only the tip as her hand worked the shaft. She felt his body tense up as he pumped in and out of her mouth faster.

"Fuck... Baby I'm about to cum... Damn Baby I'm cumming..."

His hot cum shot out of his dick down her throat with her swallowing every seed he blessed her with.

Smiling up at him she wiped her mouth with the back of her hand. "I want some more of that before the night is over."

"If you keep sucking me like that you can get that every day of the week."

Getting settled back into bed after she cleaned her mouth she thought it was time to pick Promise's brain.

"Baby, you ready to tell me what's been on your mind?"

"Doll I know this may sound crazy but I think Pops is the nigga that raped my mother."

She took a deep breath. "That's what I was thinking from the information that you told me earlier and when I thought about the way he treats you I could say he may be your father."

He turned his face up to her, "That nigga ain't my damn father he's a damn rapist."

"If it's him then yes he's a rapist but in that same token he's also your father. So when are you going to confront him about it?"

"I ain't confronting shit! That nigga is a dead man!"

She could truly understand where he was coming from. Hell she had her own father killed but Promise's case was totally different than hers and she needed him to analyze the whole situation before he did something he would regret in the end.

"Don listen I know your story and yes it's a fucked up one but think about it if Pops is your father in a sick twisted way he made sure he was a good one to you."

He looked at her like she has lost her damn mind, "I'm not understanding you right now Doll so I'm about to turn over and go to sleep. Goodnight baby."

She rubbed his back knowing her words sounded crazy to him but she needed him to understand why she spoke them.

"Don even though you may not like it that man made big Dee be a man and marry your mother. He bought your mother house and sent her enough money every month not to just take care of you but for an entire household, a husband and five children. Hell he even killed a man for her. Not to mention he basically raised you because your mother's husband sure didn't. If you think about it Pops has always been there for you. From teaching you how to ride a bike, to teaching you how to control that crazy temper of yours, to molding you into being the Kinsman County King. Everything you know about dope Pops taught you. Everything you know about stacking money Pops taught you. Everything you know about keeping your Queen in check Pops taught you."

He smiled on the inside at her last comment because she was absolutely right. Whenever he stressed about her he went straight to Pops.

She continued. "Not to mention if you kill him baby you kill our money."

"How the hell killing him has anything to do with our money. We'll just go to his connect when he's buried six feet under."

She took a deep breath before making her next statement. "Don, Pops is the connect."

He sat up in the bed and stared at her deep in her eyes "What the fuck you mean he's the connect?"

She went on to tell him the story of how Pops came to her when all of them started getting their feet wet with the heroin. He basically schooled her which in return she schooled Promise and Sincere. He made her promise that she would always protect Promise by any means necessary. He preached to her that behind every great man was a great woman and that it was her duty to make sure he didn't do knuckle head shit and fuck up like most young niggas starting out in the game did, which she has done well with so far. She went on to tell him that the first brick that he thought was fronted to them by her father's people was actually given to them by Pops and they went on from there.

Promise sat in deep thought not so much about the betrayal of Pops but how someone else must know he's the brick man and whoever that someone is may be the ones that robbed his house.

NINE

Sincere doing business with the superior nigga has been a major plus to his pockets. Seeing that much money added to his already high revenue made being away from his woman that much easier. But lately when he was around her he could feel a lot of distance between them. And for her not to even care whether he came home or not was starting to make him feel suspect. He was starting to wonder did she have a boy toy on the side.

By him being new to the relationship game sometimes he forgets to give her that extra attention that females needed. He felt as long as she was living in a nice house and he was keeping her pockets faded that was enough to show her he loves her. He has never given another female a dime of his money and trust he has many women. And he has no idea where the jealousy tendency has come from, but it's there. If Cherokee leaves the house he has to know where she's going or where she's been and for how long. If she's talking on the phone he has to know who she's talking to. If she's sleep when he comes home and doesn't care to have sex he swears she's been fucking another man. She had his mind going bananas even though they were barely seeing one another. He told himself maybe the problem was his lack of presence in their relationship and all the dirt he was doing in the streets with other females had him thinking foul about her. He was feeling so guilty about his indiscretions that he started doing sucka shit. He went through her cell phone while she was sleeping and he even questioned her daughter about their whereabouts on more than one occasion. Even as he asked her baby girl he thought to himself *this some sucka ass shit*.

All he knew was it was time for him to get his shit together. Once he handled the one business for his little sister he was going to focus more on his home life.

Cherokee sat enjoying her salad at Red Lobster with her new buddy. She would have invited Divine out to eat with her but it seemed she has been so busy lately. She actually hasn't seen her since their spa day some weeks back. And trying to get Sincere to spend some time with her was out of the question. He claims to be taking care of business but on more than one occasion she has received phone calls from women claiming how he fucked them and females bragging in the beauty shop on how he tipped x amount of dollars at the strip club. Not to mention some big booty ass broad coming to her job passing her an ultrasound picture claiming the baby is Sincere's. But does she bring all that drama to him now knowing that he has stress in the streets, no. What she does is play her position by making sure when he does decide to come home he has food waiting on him and she makes sure their house is spotless. In return all she gets is more distance and more of him accusing her of being unfaithful. So now she reasoned with herself that one outing with a friend who has a listening ear would not hurt one bit.

"So how are you going to ask me out to dinner then sit here staring off into space?"

"My bad Miss Lady, it's just I have a lot on my mind. So what's up? Tell me about your day."

Cherokee rolled her eyes, "It seems everyone have something on their mind lately."

He stared at her analyzing her comment. Everyone that was close to her has been dealing with the same problem. And by her being the only square inside the circle he knew she was feeling neglected. He held her small hand inside of his, "You know what Miss Lady you're right and from this point on when we speak to one another or when we're spending time with one another it's all about you. I promise you that."

With him speaking those words to her she could feel the sincerity in his voice making her blush on the inside. Now feeling that she could trust him and talk to him about anything she unloaded her entire relationship on him. She told him she felt like her dude wasn't focused on her anymore and how she was tired of the females making their presence known about him fucking them. She explained to him how she knows that fucking with a well-known street nigga that there were going to be some negativity going along with all the perks that she was receiving and how it was starting to weigh her down. She went on to tell him that if her and her man wasn't so distant then maybe she wouldn't be sweating the small shit. But since they were every little thing is starting to hurt her soul. She even confided in him about the cop that would visit her bank frequently and out of the blue has deposited a shit load of money.

Now she had all of his attention if she didn't at first. His ears spiked as she went on to tell him about the cop she disliked saying it was just something about his aura that was bad and how she believed that he has something to do with what she heard her man mumbling about but he won't sit down long enough to hear what she has to say. He ensured her that he was listening and she should tell him everything about the cop.

TEN

Divine decided she should pay Pops a visit. Over the years the two had become very close personally and professionally by doing business. She felt it was only right to give him the heads up about Promise. She still couldn't believe that Pops may be the man that fathered Promise but when one think about it, it seemed so perfectly clear. The way that man cared for Promise was the way a man cared for his son. If Promise would stop being a dick and open his eyes he would see how much Pops loves him and his mother.

She dialed Pops number as she pulled up in front of his house.

"Hello my beautiful Divine."

"Hello my handsome Pops." She replied loving the smoothness of his voice. "I need to talk to you about something very important."

"That's cool call me when you get here so I can come out."

"Well I'm already here but I would like to come in to talk to you."

"Now Divine you know I don't allow anyone inside my home no matter how much love I have for them."

She smiled but today that rule was going to change. "I know you don't and I know why. It's the reason why I'm here."

He looked at the phone, what does she mean by she knows why? He walked to his window and peeped out and sure enough she was sitting there.

"I doubt if you know why but anyway I'm on my way out. Give me about five minutes."

"Pops could the reason be that you don't let anyone into your home is because you have pictures of Promise and his family all around? Like I said I told you that's why I'm here."

Now he really looked at the phone crazy. How in the hell did she know about the pictures and now he was wondering did she have anything to do with the break-in of his home. Out of their entire clique she was the only one that knew he was the man with the product. Then he thought about it he knew Divine wouldn't cross him like that. Even with her deceitful ways she had lurking inside of her. One thing she wouldn't do is cross her family and they considered each other to be family.

"From your long pause I can only guess you're wondering how I know about the pictures and did I have something to do with the break-in."

"Well I'm listening."

"Pops you should know better than to think I would bring some crazy mess to your house. I know about the pictures because of your son." She knew she had his attention now.

"Hurry up and get yourself in here." Pops replied opening his front door.

She scanned the premises of Pops living room upon entry and didn't see any of the pictures that Promise said he saw. Pops must have realized that having them around was a bad move because whoever broke in his house now knew of his mini shrine of

Promise and would wonder what their relation were to one another. She found herself a place on the sofa then stared at Pops who was now seated across from her. She replayed the story that Promise had told her of how he came about to enter Pops spot and what he learned while he was in there.

"So to make a long story short Promise knows the story of his conception. Something I believe his mother regrets telling him. And you know Promise just as well as I do so you know he has no recollection of you being there for him and his family his entire life all he knows is that you raped his mother."

Pops rubbed his hands down his face and sighed. Divine smiled at the gesture because Promise does the exact same thing when he is frustrated.

She gave a slight chuckle, "Man Pops I see it so clear now I guess one would be thrown off because Promise looks so much like Innocence but now that I think about it every gesture and all his mannerisms all come from you. Even that hot temper that he has, Innocence told him about her uncle that you killed."

All he could do was shake his head. "Divine I know he has no understanding because how he was conceived was crazy. But y'all have to understand it was a different time back then. Her man had put her in an awkward situation and with me and my temper I did what I did. I'm not proud of it but it was what it was. Then the game really got fucked up. After her being there for so long my crazy ass fucked around and fell in love with her. If I could go back and change the hands of time believe me I would."

She could see the strained tears in his pretty brown eyes begging to fall but she knew Pops wouldn't allow it.

"So now my son wants to go to war with his old man huh?"

"Yeah I guess you can say that but when I explained to him of how you've been there for him and his mother his entire life I think he's reconsidering killing you. And since I told him the truth about you being the connect I guess now he's focusing on who ran up in your spot."

He had to smile at that comment. Even though his son wanted him dead he still wanted to know who had the audacity to rob him.

"Well, let him know that I've got a good idea of who came in here and I'm handling it. But you know when you said something about the pictures it through me off for a sec."

She smiled. "I knew it would. Do you care to let me know who done it?"

He stood and walked over to the door, "Not right now my beautiful Divine. All I want you to do is keep looking after my son."

With that Pops escorted her to her car and watched her go on about her way.

After her talk with Pops she decided to pick up the kids and head to the mall. It was time to bless them with some new kicks. Knowledge loved to get new tennis shoes. Every time she copped him a pair he had to leave the mall with them on his feet. She smiled to herself knowing that as soon as she put the shoes on his feet he was going to walk around looking down at them like he has never had a new pair shoes in his life. Treasure didn't care what she got as long as she was with her big brother.

On her way to Richmond Mall she decided to call and invite Cherokee and Shereé figuring they could make it an all day outing shopping, eating, and maybe a movie. Of course Cherokee agreed.

Just as she expected Knowledge walked the mall holding his sister's hand looking down at his new purple cool gray Retro 9 Air Jordan tennis shoes. They all settled in the food court getting them some Subway to eat. The children didn't care to eat their food all they wanted to do was ride the little motorized cars that sat in the middle of the food court. Which was cool because Divine and Cherokee haven't had much time to kick it with one another, so while they talked Shereé kept the dollars going in the cars. She was such a big girl.

"So how has everything been going with you and Sincere?"

Cherokee took a deep breath, "Well I couldn't really tell you. The only time I see him well should I say feel him is when he slide into bed in the middle of the night then between my legs. So I guess it's safe to say I've been having a lot of lonely days and nights."

"Kee I can honestly say I feel your pain. Promise and I have been there on many occasions. All I can really say is it's a lot going on in the streets so that's where Sin feels he needs to be. Trust me when the conflict in the streets die down he'll be back at home getting on your last nerves."

"If you say so," she responded sounding a little down.

Divine stared at her feeling just a tad bit sorry for her. She knew she wasn't built for the cons of being a street niggas main line. A lot came with that territory. Other bitches, possible kids, jail, and even death and she didn't know if Cherokee could handle that without stressing herself out. Shit she was praying that Cherokee didn't find another nigga to listen to her problems cause all that could do is lead to more problems. Divine knew that her big brother loved the hell out of his girl but he also loved the women in the streets. A small trait he picked up from their father.

"I tell you what Kee how about in a couple of weeks we take a trip to Miami I could use some South Beach sun and I'm pretty sure you could too. I know Innocence wouldn't mind babysitting for us."

"Divine you just don't know how good that sounds. I'll make sure I put in my vacation time. What you think in about a month?"

Divine thought of the time line, a month may be too soon for her, "Maybe two. That's good timing for me."

As soon as Divine finished her last statement she almost lost her breath. Coming straight towards their table was Jamal and it looked like the kids were headed towards them also.

She stood to give Jamal a hug once he reached their table. She tried to introduce him to Cherokee but she was looking like she was in some crazed daze.

"Hello earth to Cherokee."

"Oh I'm sorry I don't know where my mind wondered off to."

"I would like you to meet my good friend Jamal. Cherokee Jamal, Jamal Cherokee"

Jamal shook Cherokee's hand, "What's good with you little mama?"

The moment the words left his mouth the children ran up to them with Knowledge jumping up in his mother's arms.

"Mommy the cars go to slow, I want them to go fast." Knowledge mumbled to her.

Jamal couldn't take his eyes off Divine and the little boy who called her mommy. He didn't even know she had a kid and not to mention a kid that look like a mini light skin version of him. As he kept looking upon the little boy Jamal figured he was about two years old and now he knew why she had lost contact with him those couple of years back. He cleared his throat getting her attention.

"Um I didn't know you had a son."

Cherokee couldn't do anything but look between Knowledge and the dude Divine introduced as Jamal. She had noticed the strong resemblance the moment the guy walked up. That's why she was stuck in a daze.

Divine knew she had to defuse the situation and defuse it fast. She couldn't handle looking at Cherokee sitting there with her mouth wide open.

Sitting Knowledge down in a chair she asked Jamal could she speak to him in private.

As soon as they reached another table Jamal started in on her. "Man I'm going to come out and ask you straight up, Is your lil man mines?"

Her heart skipped about five beats before she answered. "No he's not Jamal."

"Come on now Vines he looks just like me and now I know why you disappeared some time back. Man this shit is crazy." Jamal vented getting angrier by the second.

"Jamal I can see you're getting upset so I'm going to step off but like I told you before he's not your son."

She attempted to walk away but Jamal quickly pulled her back by her arm.

"Vines I know I joke around with you a lot but this shit right here isn't a laughing matter. Any nigga with eyes could see that's me, even your girl sitting over there with her mouth wide open looking like she got the shock of her life. What you got her thinking someone else is his fuckin' daddy?"

"Jamal it's complicated." She replied as she tried to pull away from his grasp.

Pulling her even closer to him he stated, "Well simplify it for me then."

ELEVEN

Diamond couldn't believe how gone Detective Barns had her. Maybe it was his age because she has never gotten a feeling like this from someone in her age range. Now she could honestly say that she was in love. He made her feel as if she was number one in his life. For once she didn't have to come second to Divine. Yeah she cared for her fake sister but Promise made it feel like she was the Queen of everything and not just him. Anything she said was law. Now what part of the game was that? If he had an idea and Divine didn't like it, it was operation shut down. To her Promise was one of the toughest niggas she knew, but when it came to his precious Queen the nigga needed to grow some balls. Yeah when he first wanted her to get close to Detective Barns some time back it was for information but now she didn't regret when she decided on her own to sleep with him.

She had already known that the money he got from his last bust was Divine's but she didn't care. It was Divine's money not her brother's money which made the case totally different in her eyes. Barns had never told her that the bust was on Buckeye he came straight out telling her it was some young nigga on Cedar that was on the rise but of course he didn't know she knew of the young cat. Most of the money he got from the bust he spent on her. Now the product was a totally different story. The majority of that was going straight up his nose. And that may be the only problem with their relationship. She didn't care if he was tooting his own nose but to keep trying to get her to try was getting on her last nerve. If there was one thing she has learned from her brother and his Queen was not to do drugs, no way no how.

Diamond thought she would pay her man a visit before she went to her mother's house. She knew she would find him locked up in his house because he hasn't been to work in weeks. She was starting to believe that he has gotten himself fired. She opened the door with the key that he had given her. She walked directly to his bedroom and wasn't shocked at all at what she saw upon entry. He was standing in front of his dresser with only his underwear on preparing his next line of heroin. Never acknowledging her presence he leaned down and snorted the line up one nostril then snorted another line up the other. He leaned his head back pitching his nose to ensure that he would get a good drain down the back of his throat. That's the part he enjoyed the most, the drain. Satisfied with the drain he acknowledged his young beautiful girlfriend.

"Hey baby I was hoping I was going to see you today." He stated with a slur in his voice.

"Yeah I've been missing you so I decided to drop by. You've been locked up in this house for a couple of days now."

"That I have, you know I've got a lot on my mind. Also I just wanted to stay in and relax before my vacation was over."

"Vacation, I didn't know you were on vacation."

She never got a reply from her last statement because the drug was starting to take effect on him. He made his way to sit on the edge of the bed to enjoy the beautiful feel of a nod.

Instead of standing there watching him drift in and out of lala land she decided to straighten up his house then head to her mother's.

TWELVE

Cherokee eyes rolled in the top of her head as she enjoyed the feeling of getting her pussy ate. She would not have thought in a million years that the young dude she has been confiding in will give her the best head she has ever had. True Sincere's tongue action was the bomb and has brought her more organisms than she could count but this little nigga head game was the truth. Every lick and every suck he did was with much precision bringing her to the best orgasm she has ever had. She didn't know if it was the orgasm or the guilt of letting someone else taste her other than Sincere but a thousand tears was streaming down her face. Her heart felt so heavy, which let her know it was the guilt she was feeling. Once he attempted to enter her she came to her senses.

"I am so sorry, but I can't do this."

She tried to get from under her friend but he pushed her back down.

"What the fuck you mean you can't do this? But you can lie there and let me eat your pussy though, huh? Man you got me fucked up, you giving me some pussy."

She then went ballistic trying to fight him off of her. She tried and tried to push him off but he was just too strong for her. He grabbed her hands forcibly holding them together above her head with one hand then shoved his dick inside of her with the other.

Who the fuck did she think she was telling me I couldn't get any pussy after her punk ass came all over my face. Who the fuck did she think she was playing with. What woman gets ass naked alone with a man allow him to eat her pussy then all of sudden grow a conscious saying she can't do it. Where the fuck did they do that at? He said to himself as he pounded his dick in and out of her with much force.

Cherokee mind instantly went blank the moment he entered her. She could not believe in a million years that she was being raped. True she had every intention on having sex with him when she first got there, but she changed her mind. She no longer wanted to betray the man she loves with all her heart. Now she regretted ever having a conversation with this guy, she regretted going out to dinner with him on her lonely nights, and she damn sure regretted going to his apartment and allowing him to taste her private area that belongs to Sincere. The rape wasn't even where her concern was anymore, Sincere was going to fucking kill her. She was brought back to reality from his weight being lifted off of her.

"Damn you got some good pussy." He exclaimed rolling over and rubbing her thigh.

She looked over at him like he was crazy. What part of what he did make him think everything was cool. She jumped out of bed threw her clothes on to rush home and wash away her sins. She cried her entire drive home.

To her surprise when she entered her home Sincere was sitting on the couch watching his favorite show True Blood.

When he pressed pause on the DVR to greet her only thing he saw was her clothes all out of place on her body. He stood slowly and began to walk over in her direction even slower.

She saw hatred and pain in his eyes and knew where his mind was roaming to. She walk away heading towards the bathroom before he could get to close to her. Before she could get her foot into the bathroom door good she felt him yank her by her hair.

He turned her to him to get a good look at her face before he punched her in it and that's when he saw it. It was fear but not so much fear of him. He took a step back to access the situation. He could tell she had been crying, her hair was all over head, and her clothes was thrown on her body any kind of way. He could clearly see that someone has violated his woman. He kissed her swollen lips silently apologizing to her for not being there for her. He began to undress her slowly listening to her quiet sobs. He sat her on the sink then opened her legs so he could take a look at her vagina. What he saw hurt his soul. Her pussy was so red and swollen like someone had fucked her with no remorse. He looked at her teary beautiful face then began to shed tears himself. He lifted her off the sink then began to run her some bath water. After the bath was ready he placed her in the tub then joined her by sitting behind her hugging her tightly.

"Who did this to you Kee Baby?"

She began to cry all over again which sent sharp pains through Sincere's heart.

"Baby I'm sorry this happened to you but I can't do anything if you don't talk to me."

"I don't know who he was." She blurted out with tears and snot running down her face.

He turned her to him smothering her face in his chest. "This is all my fault. I haven't been around to protect you and I am so sorry Baby. I promise you this will never happen to you again. I'm not letting you out of my sight anymore and tomorrow the first thing we're going to do is get you a gun. You're going to learn how to protect yourself for the times I can't be around. Do you understand me?"

She shook her head yes in his chest.

"Kee I have a serious question to ask you. Did he use a condom?"

She cried even harder shaking her head no in his chest.

The next question he asked was going to hurt him more than it did her. He breathed heavily, "Did he release inside of you?"

She shook her head yes one again. From that answer they both now sat in the bathtub shedding tears.

"Baby I'm going to take you to Planned Parent Hood tomorrow so we can get you that plan B pill okay."

Crying some more she answered, "Okay. I'm so sorry Sincere, Baby I swear I am."

"It's going to be okay, I promise you that."

He held her in his arms for what felt like eternity.

Sincere eased out of bed once he thought Cherokee was sleeping. He went down to his man cave to think. Someone has violated his woman meaning someone had to pay. After sitting in deep thought for about an hour he picked up the phone to give his sister a call.

Divine looked at Sincere's name come across the screen then looked at the time. She knew something was definitely wrong.

"What's wrong Twin?" She asked answering her phone.

"Some bullshit"

She knew he needed to talk. She tapped Promise on the shoulder letting him know she was going to the living room.

"Talk to me big bro."

He told her the entire story of what transpired from the moment Cherokee arrived home.

"Damn Sin that's fucked up. She absolutely don't have any idea of who did this to her?"

"That's the thing Doll, yes I could clearly see that someone forced themselves on her but as I hold her in my arms my heart is telling me that it's more to it. That's why I need you."

"Say no more, I'll get it out of her."

"Thanks Doll."

"Yup"

With that they ended the call and both headed back to bed.

Cherokee felt when Sincere left the bed and felt when he returned because she was wide awake. Sleep would not be her friend that night. She lay in his arms hating that she had to lie to him. Yes she was raped but if he'd known she put herself in the fucked up situation she knew he would have never forgiven her. And she couldn't possibly tell him who the accused was. She could not by any means be the cause of him and his best friend falling out.

Divine phone rang again an hour after she had drifted off into a deep sleep. This time it was Jay calling.

"It better be good." She answered upset that her sleep was broken for the second time.

"It is! I got the whereabouts of where those dirty cops lay their heads."

"Yup" was her only reply before hanging up the phone then going back to sleep for the night.

THIRTEEN

It has been an entire month since Jamal had seen Divine at the mall and an entire month of her spinning him about her getting a paternity test for her son. Since she wanted to play games he had some games for her ass. Maybe because he was so nice to her she thought he was soft or something but it was about time for her to check his resume because he was something like a gangster.

He pulled up in front of her grandmother's house then gave her call.

"I'm sitting outside your grandmother's house I would advise you to get down here so we can talk."

Divine looked at her phone like what the fuck. "Boy please you don't even know where my grandmother stays."

"Yellow house down on 82nd and Quincy, if I wanted to I could go to the window to get a bottle of liquor so like I said get down here so we can talk."

How the hell did Jamal know where her grandmother lived she had no idea. Divine knew she was wrong for dodging him but what the hell did he think was supposed to happen? Picture her trying to tell Promise that she knew all along that Rob wasn't her baby daddy and his real father is the nigga in EC he saw her with. He would swear up and down that she was still fucking the nigga which wasn't the case. To Promise she had only had sex with two men him and Rob but if she would let him know about Jamal also she knows he would begin to interrogate about everything she has done and she damn sure wasn't ready for that. Hell neither was he for real.

She pulled up in front of her grandmother's house making it down there in record time. She hopped inside of Jamal's car with evil written all over her face.

"First of all Jamal I don't appreciate you threatening me. Second of all how the hell do you know where my grandmother stays?"

"Slow your roll Vines, don't get in my car with all that yin yang shit. I told you to get at me over a month ago and since you didn't I can see you're really hiding something. All I ask was to get a paternity test, if he's not mine then we're cool, but if he is you have a lot of explaining to do."

"Jamal like I told you at the mall it's complicated."

He looked at her, "And like I told you at the mall simplify that shit then. I mean like for real Vines you have come over to my mother's house and kicked it with her on numerous occasions sat in her face laughing and giggling and shit like everything sweet. Like you ain't got her grandbaby stashed away somewhere." He threw his hands up in the air, "Fuck! You in my face like we fucking best friends or some shit and ain't told me I could possibly be a fuckin' father. What part of the game is that?"

She looked over at him knowing she was dead wrong. But she had good reason. Her not telling him was for his own good. Yeah she was wrong leading Promise and Rob on making them think that Rob was the father but she knew Promise would be watching her every move which meant death of whoever her child's father was. Yeah she was also wrong for playing with Rob's life like that but now she says fuck it. He got what the fuck he deserves. But what she didn't want was any harm to come to Jamal. He was too good of a nigga for that.

"Okay Jamal it's like this, my dude ain't wrapped to tight in the head and he has no idea that I was sleeping with you so it's safe to say me not telling you about my son was only for your protection."

He looked at her and laughed. "Your dude ain't wrapped to tight, my protection, who the fuck do you think I am. I ain't no fuckin' punk and I damn sure ain't scared of no fuckin' Promise. Yeah you thought I didn't know who your dude was. Well I do and that nigga bleed just like me. I'm going to be in my son's life and if that nigga get out of pocket I have no problem laying that nigga out. So when are you bringing my son to see me?"

She stared at him with her facial expression saying (what the fuck). How in the hell did he know about Promise? Where did she get all these stalking ass men from?

"Divine you can stop the wheels from spinning in your head and answer my question. When are you bringing my son to spend some time with me?"

"I'll bring him this Saturday coming up."

He started his car and politely asked her to get the fuck out but not before letting her know that if he had to come find her again it was going to be problems for her and her man.

She decided to leave the kids at their grandmother's house so she and Promise could have some alone time. She figured she would cook a home cooked meal since she hasn't been in the kitchen in weeks. Also so she could cushion the blow on the news she was going to be giving him.

She prepared salmon crockets over a bed of wild rice with gravy drizzled on top, a tossed garden salad with Ken's Country French dressing. She also made a pitcher of his favorite Kool-Aid, tropical punch.

After putting the finishing touches on dinner she texted him

Me: Home now!
Don: On my way!

When Promise entered his home he knew something was up once he saw the dinner spread on the dining room table instead of the kitchen. His theory was confirmed when he saw the glass pitcher of his favorite Kool-Aid. His Queen hated for him to drink it said it had too much sugar in it that he didn't need. And then to top everything else, his Queen was sitting at the head of the dinner table looking like the Boss Bitch that she was. Her body was laced in a black and white tuxedo looking bra with the matching French cut panty that was straining to cover her fat ass. On her feet were some black patent leather peep-toe four inch red bottom pumps.

She took the moment to stand to greet her man. "Welcome home Daddy!"

He gave her his sinister smile, "What did I do to deserve this tonight?"

"The question you should be asking is what you don't do," she replied as she helped him settle in his chair.

Trailing his finger along the lace of her panty he asked, "Mmm hmm, what if I tell you salmon isn't the fish I have a taste for?"

"I would tell you that the salmon is just the appetizer and I would be serving the main course in our bedroom."

"Well if that's the case you may serve me then."

He didn't make it halfway through his wonderful dinner before she decided to have the big talk.

"Daddy I have something very important I want to discuss with you."

Still enjoying his food he told her, "I figured that much once I walked through the door. So speak."

"Well I really don't know where to start so I guess I'll get straight to it. Rob wasn't Knowledge's real father. I have my reasons for letting you believe that he was but that's neither here or there, what's important for me to tell you is his real father knows about him and wants to be involved in his life."

He looked at the love of his life like she has lost her fucking mind. What the fuck did she mean Rob wasn't the real father? And if he wasn't who the fuck was? And where the fuck did the nigga come from, thin air.

"All I need to know is the nigga's name and where he resides," Promise stated with much malice in his voice.

She knew that was going to be the first thing that was going to come out of his mouth and she was also prepared for it, but what she didn't expect was the look on his face. He looked like he was possessed or some shit. The facial expression he was giving her was making her wish that she never had opened up her mouth at all. As long as she has known him and has known of his crazy ways she has never been afraid of him, but she couldn't say that now. And even though she was scared shitless she was going to hold her ground.

"That's not important Don. What's important is he's going to be involved in our son's life without any harm coming to him."

Promise stood up from his seat. He walked slowly over to where she was sitting. He stood over her staring down at her.

"Don I know..............."

Before she could finish her sentence he grabbed her throat silencing her words.

"What the fuck is the niggas name and where the fuck does he reside? That is the only thing I want to hear come out yo' muthafuckin' mouth. Do you fuckin' understand me?" He then released the hold he had on her neck so she could tell him what he wanted to hear.

She tried to stand in her chair but he wasn't having that shit. He pushed her back down just as fast as she tried to stand up.

She scooted back in her chair, which was not far at all, holding her neck. She could not believe he had put his hands on her. *This is not happening* was all she could think to herself. She decided she would try to reason with him because he was obviously not acting like himself.

"Don, just…."

Whop…. was the only thing heard from the vicious slap he laid across her left cheek sending her tumbling out of her chair.

"His name ain't no fucking Don just. Now what the fuck is the nigga's name Divine Nanette and stop fuckin' playing wit' me."

Since she was on the floor she knew she had to make a run for it. He was showing her a side of him that she wasn't prepared for. All she had to do was make it to their bedroom and retrieve her baby nine. No she didn't want to shoot him but he was giving her no other choice. She stood up from the floor trying to make a run for it but he stopped her dead in her tracks by grabbing her by the back of her neck then body slamming her down on the dining room table.

"Uhhhhhh," she screamed out in pain. She could feel blood trickling down her back but was too afraid to feel behind her fearing that a knife was in her back.

He stood her up holding her by her neck. He stared at her seeing nothing but fear something he has never seen in her. He stared even harder hating what she made him do to her. He has known for the past couple of months that something was up with his son so why did he react the way he did when all she was trying to do was come clean and be honest. He untangled his fingers from around her neck. He wrapped his strong arms around her smothering her face in his chest.

"Baby Doll I am so sorry. I am so sorry for putting my hands on you. You know I didn't mean that shit. I don't know what the fuck just came over me. Please forgive me."

Divine was awakened with the sun beaming through the window on her bruised face and with Promise pulling her closer into his arms. The last thing she could remember was him bathing her apologizing over and over again about how sorry he was for putting his hands on her. She couldn't recall getting into bed nor did she remember falling asleep.

She tried to get out of bed but he stopped her. "Where you going Doll?"

She closed her eyes and exhaled heavily, "I'm going to the bathroom to take a shower so I can get dressed to go get my babies."

He pulled her even closer to him, "Come on now Doll you know I can't let my babies see you like this. I already called Innocence and told her she was going to have to watch them for a couple of days."

She sighed. "Well I guess I'm only going to use the bathroom then."

She sat on the toilet trying to recall the last night events after Promise whooped her ass but for the life of her she couldn't remember anything. She hated when her mind went blank. It had to be because of the wine she was sipping on before he had gotten home. Instead of dwelling on it she took care of her business in the bathroom then climbed back into bed snuggling against him. She cried silent tears in his chest hating what she had saw in the bathroom mirror. The left side of her face was swollen with the worst looking black eye she has ever seen.

Divine hated being in the house but she didn't have any other choice. Promise was not allowing anyone to see his Queen's face all fucked up.

For the past three days that she was trapped she battled, more so with herself than with Promise. She couldn't believe she had made it seem okay that he physically put his hands on her and that was saying it mildly because he downright beat her ass. She didn't care how mad he had gotten he should not have laid a finger on her, not her Promise. His only roll was to protect her, mentally and physically. With him she was supposed to be safe, even if he wasn't wrapped to tight. His hostility has never been towards her, his possessiveness yes but never his hostile ways. But how did she honestly think his possessiveness wasn't going to turn physical one day. She also knew she was dead wrong for using his aggressive ways for her own benefits. She knew when she was getting the attention that she thought she needed during her pregnancy from Rob, that his life was limited. It just so happen he didn't deserve his life. His ass was just as crazy as Promise. And now she sees a little crazy in Jamal ass also. Why the hell did she attract the psycho paths? Why she asked herself that question she didn't know because she knew why. The crazy ones always flocked to her because she was just as crazy as they were. She really had to be if she was staying with Promise after he swelled her face up, making her look like the elephant man's wife. Well it was what it was. She wasn't going anywhere and they both knew that. Now there she sat in the house secluded from the outside world just like a battered woman.

Even though she didn't like being held hostage she did appreciate the quality time that they were spending with one another. Yes they lived in the same house and yes Promise stayed between her legs but she couldn't recall the last time that they have cuddled and watched movies together. With the cuddling they also discussed what he expected from her, nothing about what she expected, typical Promise.

He informed her that the only reason she was going to get a pass with his son and his so called biological father Jamal was because she and Promise wasn't together when she had gotten pregnant. He also informed her that she was going to bless him with a young God of his own even though his love for Knowledge would never change. So it was safe to say that he flushed her birth control down the toilet. Last but not least he informed her that there were only two options with the two of them, they were going to be either married or buried. She politely accepted the married because she knew her boo was a killer for real.

Divine really didn't have a problem with his list of demands because her Don was a boss and she knew it wasn't another nigga on the face of the earth that can tame her and her ways. And seeing as though her Don was such a boss she had no problem letting him know that her brother Jay knew the whereabouts of her dope and her money. Messing around with him she might be waking up to her shit first thing in the morning.

FOURTEEN

Promise watched from a far as his little sister interacted with the crooked cop. The way she was fawning over him was beginning to make him sick to his stomach. He was starting to wonder was he going to have to kill his sister also from the way she acting with the nigga. He didn't want to kill the bum ass cop and his sister gets to talking because she got caught up in her feelings. There was one thing for sure and two for certain jail was not an option for him. Leave his Queen on the streets with all those sucka ass niggas, fuck no! After observing the two together he knew he would have to take care of the cop without his sister's knowledge or anyone else's for that matter. The last thing he wanted to do was send another one of his siblings to meet their maker because they got in their feelings.

"Weakness number one - young pussy, weakness number two - dope, didn't muthafucka's know that being so open with their weaknesses was going to be their down fall." He spoke to himself not believing how easy the detective was going to make it for him to kill his junkie ass.

***

Jay opened his front door greeting Promise with a head nod.

After returning the gesture Promise made himself comfortable on Jay's plush sofa.

"I see you eating real good around here," Promise stated as he admired the couch.

"Yeah I'm doing pretty good."

"Damn nigga you ain't go offer yo' boy nothing to drink?"

"My bad P I'll grab you a bottle of water out the fridge. I know you don't do that pop and juice shit too much."

"I'm glad you didn't have anything to do with the shit that happened at your spot," Promise mentioned after retrieving the water from Jay.

"I told y'all in the beginning that I ain't have shit to do with it, but I guess I can see how it looked like I did. It really doesn't matter now since we know the truth. But on some real shit P that nigga Sincere, never mind man I'll keep my comments to myself," Jay said shaking his head making himself mad all over again.

Promise raised one eyebrow looking at him sideways. He took note of the tension that was coming off him as he spoke of Sincere's name.

"Well if you got some ill comments about my peeps I do suggest you keep that shit to yourself, but um let me get that address."

Jay pulled out the address to Detective Barns home then handed it to Promise.

"How did you get this anyway?"

"Guess I'll keep that lil' bit of information to myself as well." Jay responded loving the fact the he had one up on the so called Fam.

◆◆◆◆◆◆

The next person on Promise's visiting list for the day was Pops. He no longer wanted to murder the man due to Divine's over understanding ass. She could be a trip sometimes, if someone was in her circle they could do no wrong, but if they wasn't she didn't give two flying fucks about them, "off with their heads", she would sometimes say. He guessed Pops should be thankful because he was definitely part of Divine's circle which meant hands off for Promise. Hearing the way she pleaded Pops case one could argue that she knew all along about their relation to one another.

Pops waited patiently by his front door waiting for Promise to pull up. He figured there was no reason for him to meet him outside because they were way past that point. There will be no more hiding from his only son. Whatever Promise wanted to know he would be happy to give him an honest answer. He only prayed that his son was coming to talk and not go to war, because if he truly had to he would kill his one and only child. Therefore his trusty glock 9mm will stay nestled on his hip in case shit got serious.

Promise had to sit in his car just a little while longer to get his thoughts together. Last thing he wanted was to go against his word and do something drastic to his ole man. Once he felt he was good he exited his car and walked onto Pops porch.

After standing face to face staring at each other for at least two minutes the two finally embraced with a hug.

Standing to the side Pops invited his son into his home, "Come on in and have a seat Promise."

Promise sat on the sofa taking in the scenery. "I see you got rid of the pictures."

"Not so much got rid of them just put them away for safe keeping. I know who came in here took notice and I know they're doing a lot of wondering themselves."

"Yeah speaking of that, so you figured out who it was that invaded your space?"

Pops couldn't help but smile at his son. He knew Promise was asking so he could take care of them but he wasn't going to let his son take care of his light work.

"Yeah I know exactly who it was and I'm handling it right now as we speak. Actually I'm killing two birds with one stone."

"What do you mean by that?" Promise asked with his usual screwed up face.

"Hold that thought P let me go grab us something to drink."

Pops returned from the kitchen with two bottles of purified water.

"Okay you asked what do I mean but let me ask you something first. Have you ever wondered why you and your crew never been investigated or harassed by the local police?"

Promise thought about his question for a second, "No I've never wondered why I just figured we were being extra careful."

"Well I guess I can give y'all that. I can honestly say that y'all are extremely careful. But still with all the crime and money that's going through these forties don't you think someone would have taken notice?"

"Damn Pops I guess I never thought of that."

"Well when y'all first started out y'all young asses was ringing a lot of bells. That's when I pulled Baby Doll to the side telling her how to straighten that shit up and I've been coaching her along the way ever since. I also had a friend on the task force unit that I paid handsomely to keep his people blind to what was going on over here which wasn't that hard because I was only protecting what was going on in the forties. Therefore whatever happened in the thirties and fifties was enough to keep the police main focus. That was until some crooked cop on their unit started getting greedy which made him start a little investigation on his own that lead him straight to me."

Promise stopped him from talking because he now had an important question of his own. "Doll told me that you was the connect all this time so what did they actually get out of your house?"

Pops gave a slight chuckle to his question, "Come on now son I live over here by choice not force which means they didn't get a damn thing out of here. This is just a spot I keep to be close to you and your mother. I do have another home and I have totally different spot where I warehouse my product. You think I can give Baby Doll all that game if I didn't know what the hell I was doing? But back to what I was saying the same crooked cop that came up in my spot was the same one that hit Doll's little brother spot down on Cedar. Of course he didn't know that was Kinsman County dope, he only saw a young boy on the rise and decided to take his shot."

"Pops you might be right because I saw them niggas down on Cedar long before Doll had her brother take over. Those niggas already planned on going down there but shit became even sweeter when Jay took over. But you said you was killing two birds with one stone what did you have in mind?"

"My plan has been in motion since y'all put Diamond on him," Pops replied showcasing the same sinister smile that Promise usually has.

"Well Pops I don't know what your plan is but I'm praying you're not putting my sister in harm's way, her ass on some bullshit anyway. But like I said before I'm handling it."

Pops shook his head at his only son. "I would never put Diamond in harm's way and don't you ever suggest that I would. And she ain't on no bullshit, she's doing exactly what I told her to do."

"What! What do you mean she's doing what you told her to do?"

"Like I said before relax Promise your old man got this."

With that being said Pops patted Promise on his right shoulder then retired to his bedroom leaving his son to let himself out.

FIFTEEN

Cherokee's guilty conscious was starting to get the best of her. She could hardly stay focused at work during the day nor could she get a good rest during the night. With Sincere being around her so much was making her feel even guiltier. He took her to work, picked her up on her lunch breaks, and one day when he picked her up at the end of the day he stayed in the house with her for the rest of the evening. She hated knowing that she lied to him. True she was raped but she couldn't help but to feel as if it was all her fault. She keeps telling herself that if she wasn't there in the first place that it would have never happened. Sometimes she wants to tell Sincere the truth and let it be the guy's word against hers but she couldn't afford for him to fall out with his best friend. She reasoned with herself that they were best friends before she came along and she knew very well that they would be best friends long after she and Sincere couldn't stand the sight of each other any longer. Seeing as though she was having a mental breakdown she decided she would pay Divine a visit. She hasn't seen her in a couple of weeks and was missing her new found friend. She basically wanted to feel some female energy even if it was only for a couple of hours.

She tapped Sincere on his shoulder, "Babe I think I'm going to go visit Divine today. Maybe spend a couple of hours with her. We haven't seen each other in a couple of weeks."

Sincere lay on his side thinking that may be a wonderful idea. One reason being that he wanted Divine to pull some information from Cherokee from the night she was raped and the second being he needed some time away from Cherokee. He needed him a taste of Sensual.

"Yeah that sounds like a good idea. I'll drop you off over there then pick you up later on tonight."

Divine slide open the patio door that lead to the balcony outside of her bedroom. She watched Promise as he sat in deep thought. After admiring him for a short time she decided to join him. She sat down next to him on the patio couch gazing at the backyard. She loved the scenery of her backyard especially during the autumn months. September and October were her favorite months of the year they weren't too hot or too cold. She loved looking at the trees as their leaves changed colors and not to mention she got to wear all her wedged Timberland boots and her many crop style jackets.

Looking out at her spacious yard she envisioned her and the children running around playing. They too enjoyed the autumn months. She would rake the leaves in large piles then she and the kids would jump into them rolling around on the ground.

Staring out at the backyard she spoke with sincerity in voice, "I miss my babies Don."

Never looking in her direction, "I know you do. Give your eye a couple of more days to heal then I'll go pick them up."

Even though that wasn't what she wanted she knew it was for the best. Her eye was still a light shade of purple and she knew it wouldn't be good for her children to see her face that way.

"You're right I just miss them. Can you please promise me nothing like this will ever happen between us again? I mean I love you Don but I will not allow you to put your hands on me because you can't control your temper." Now staring deeply in his eyes, "I refuse to go to war with someone that I will kill and die for."

"I agree," was his only response before getting up and leaving her on the balcony alone with her thoughts.

Divine sat on the balcony for all of five minutes before she started freezing. As she stepped through the patio door Promise was greeting her with her cell phone. She looked at the screen noticing he had answered it. She thought *oh no the fuck he didn't*.

"Oh yes the fuck I did," Promise said out loud then turned to walk out of the bedroom.

She smiled and shook her head then turned her attention to her cell, "What's good Kee?"

"Nothing much, just missing my new friend that's all." Cherokee responded sounding a little down.

"Awe I miss you too. What have you been up to?"

"Well I was thinking I would come spend the day with you then I'll give you all the updates."

"Yeah that's cool. What time are you coming?"

"I should be there within an hour and a half."

"Okay I'll see you when you get here."

Since Cherokee was coming to visit Divine decided she would make them some lunch. She fried up some tilapia, baked some potatoes, and tossed a spinach salad. Her beverage of choice was pink bubbly moscoto. She figured they would watch movies so she set out all the Fridays, all of Katt Williams stand ups, and all of Kevin Hart stand ups. And she rolled them up two sticks of loud. If they didn't do anything else they were going to laugh.

By the time Cherokee arrived Divine had transformed her living room into a straight camp. Any and every thing they should need was right there at their fingertips.

The first thing Cherokee noticed when she walked through the door was Divine's eye.

"Girl what the hell happened to your eye?"

"I had a little disagreement with Promise. But we cool now."

With much sincerity in her voice Cherokee asked, "Are you sure?"

"Girl I'm positive. It ain't shit me and my Don go through that I can't handle you can trust and believe that."

Cherokee shrugged her shoulders, "If you say so."

After they finished their food, about two glasses of wine, and one blunt Divine noticed Cherokee didn't laugh at one of Kevin Hart's jokes. Now she knew no one in their right frame of mind could watch that retarded

Negro and not laugh. Especially Cherokee seeing as though she laughed at anything.

"What's good Kee? What got you all serious over there?"

"Nothing really, just got a lot on my mind."

From the sound of her voice Divine could tell she truly indeed had a lot on her mind then she remember the incident that Sincere had told her about. She decided now would be a good time to do some prying.

"I can hear in your voice that something is bothering you and that something must be the reason you wanted to spend the day over here so gone and let it out."

"Well dag Vine, you don't have to sound too sincere about it."

"I'm sorry Kee I'm not that good with my soft consoling side, but gone head and let it out."

After taking about a thousand deep breaths Cherokee unloaded her worst nightmare. She told her how she was feeling neglected by Sincere and how she knew he was fucking everything moving. She explained how she came about meeting a friend that she soon started to spend time with. She assured her that it was nothing more than a few lunches and dinners with a whole lot of laughs. Then she finally made it to that frightful night when she was violated, making sure she let Divine know that Sincere only knows about the rape and not the friendship she had formed with the guy.

By the time she finished her story Divine was shedding a few tears showing her soft side. She hated to hear about a woman being violated. True Cherokee was wrong for being over that nigga's house but Divine chalked it up to her being lonely. Not every woman could handle having a nigga that ran the streets and still played in a lot of pussy that was out there in those streets. But once she told that nigga "NO" that should have been the end of that, with no ifs, ands, or buts about it. The nigga violated and not just any female but her brother's female, whoever the nigga was he had to go.

"Cherokee I'm going to ask you this one time and one time only, what's the nigga's name? I promise you I will not tell Sincere, I'm going to handle everything myself. But I need the nigga's name and his whereabouts."

Cherokee shook her head slowly. "See that's the thing Vine I can't tell you or anyone else for that matter. It's just a little too close to home."

"Man Kee I don't care about none of that too close to home shit, the nigga violated so has to go."

"For real Divine I can't tell you. I only told you the story so I could get some of the guilt off my chest and to have a good friend to listen to me. But I promise you if I could I would tell you who he was in a heartbeat, but I just can't."

She stared at Cherokee intensely, "Well if that's how you feel, I can't help but respect that."

For the rest of Cherokee's stay Divine couldn't help but wonder who the guy was. That comment to close to home was starting to get to her.

SIXTEEN

While Divine was held up in the house Promise took that as an open invitation to spend time with his west side boo Trish. Even though he worshipped the ground Divine walked on he couldn't get enough of Trish. She possessed some things that Divine didn't have femininity and neediness.

Whenever he called Divine on the phone she answered with "What's up?" or "What's good?" Some days she even threw in a "Speak!" Very not lady like to him but whenever he called Trish he was always greeted with "Hey Baby, I was just thinking about you." All Divine did was run the streets chasing a dollar. He damn near had to handcuff her to the stove to get a home cooked meal out of her but with Trish she texted him every day telling him what she had cooked rather he made it over there to eat was something different, but the action of her cooking everyday was always there. Divine's house clothes of choice consisted of his oversized shirts with some type of bottoms, be it stretch pants or basketball shorts on the other hand with Trish she always walked around the house in booty shorts even though she didn't have a whole lot of ass to hang out like Divine's but it was still nice to see her half naked the days he did drop by. What he liked most about Trish was the fact that she needed him. He liked a woman that needed him to put gas in her car or needed him to leave money on the table for bills and groceries. Bottom line was he liked to feel needed. With Divine he knew she didn't need him for a thing. If he didn't pay the bills he knew she would have no problem paying them out of her own pocket. She probably had more money in her stash then he did so he knew she didn't need him for anything. He also knew she couldn't help being who she was. She was raised to be a hustler and to be independent. She ran with him and Sincere all day every day since she was twelve years of age so her being a little rough around the edges was kind of a given. It was part of her Gemini personality because when she did show her soft feminine side he would trail behind her like a sad puppy dog. He loved days when he would come home and she would be cooking in the kitchen with her bra and panties and a sexy pair of heels on. If he could get that side of her everyday he wouldn't dare look at another woman. Well he could say if she also learned the little trick that Trish did with her tongue while she gave him head he would really be focused on his Queen and his Queen alone.

Trish hopped out of the bed after receiving Promise's text message letting her know he would be arriving at her house shortly. She stuffed her sweat pants and large T-shirt that she was wearing in the laundry baskets then jumped in the shower. Once she was out of the shower she lotion her body quickly and slid on a pair of LOVE PINK booty shorts with the matching tank top then hurried to the kitchen to see what food she had that was quick to prepare.

The first time Promise tried to holla at Trish she knew she had hit the jack pot. Even with him lying to her saying his name was Rico. He had no recollection of going to elementary school with her but she remembered everything about him. From his crooked tie his mother had put on him for their first grade class picture to his now so called Queen Baby Doll. As much as she loved him she hated how he was so brutally open and honest about his home life. He had let it be known from the gate that under no circumstance was he ever going to leave his Queen. And she tried every trick in the book to out shine his precious woman but he didn't budge. She still had hope though. For some reason he couldn't stay out of her house and out of her bed so his Queen had to be slacking in some area of their relationship.

Trish like most children on Kinsman grew up in a single family home with that single parent being addicted to crack cocaine. She was the child that no other children paid attention to or wanted to interact with because of her appearance. She also never tried to make any friends because of her appearance. The thing was she never knew anything different. She wasn't one of the children who had a good life then when the crack epidemic hit everything hit rock bottom. She was the child that was born to a mother that had done one type of drug or another for her entire life. She hated her life. The only thing that gave her childhood any comfort was day dreaming about the light skin boy with the pretty brown eyes, Promise Green. As a teenager her main focus was graduating high school and going to college so she could get a good job so she would be able to take care of herself and want for nothing, then the light skin boy would finally notice her. Now as an adult she has accomplished her goals finishing school and landing herself a wonderful job and even snagging the light skin boy's attention with one obstacle in her way, his Queen.

Promise entered Trish's house to the smell of pork chops being fried. He stepped inside the kitchen and stared at the back of her head as she flipped a piece of the swine.

Trish could feel him staring at her so she peeked over her right shoulder with a sexy smile on her face. "Hey Baby, I'm almost done. You can go to the bathroom to wash up and about time you get back your feast will be complete."

He raised his right eyebrow, "What the fuck are you cooking?"

His expression and the tone of his voice through her off she looked at the stove then back at him, "I'm cooking pork chops. Why?"

He shook his head then walked out of the kitchen. He sat down on the couch and started his usual channel surfing.

She prepared Promise's plate of fried pork chops, garlic mashed potatoes, cheese broccoli, and a diner roll. She placed his plate on the cocktail table with a big glass of orange Kool-Aid. She sat down next to him after returning from the kitchen with her plate of food and noticed he hasn't touched his plate.

"Babe, what's wrong? You haven't touched your food yet."

Staring blankly at the television he responded, "What food are you referring to?"

She didn't comprehend where the conversation was headed because clearly his food was sitting in front of him on the table.

"Um the food that's sitting on the table."

Now he was staring directly at her as if she was the dumbest person on the face of the earth. "I hope you're not referring to the plate of swine that you sat down in front of me knowing that I don't eat no damn pork."

"Oh my God Baby I am so sorry I completely forgot. I was just trying to fix something real quick because you were on your way. Let me go fix you something else."

"Nawl, that won't be necessary." He began to unfasten his belt buckle and his pants. "Just give me a shot of head real quick."

She started smiling from ear to ear. She loved giving him head. She could tell from his reactions that he wasn't getting his dick suck like a pro at home. Getting on her knees she replied, "Anything you say Daddy."

Promise came within five minutes flat from the head job she gave him making sure she swallowed every single baby that he shot down her throat.

She stood up in front of him smiling sensually asking "How was that Daddy?"

He gave a slight smirk then buttoned up his pants and proceeded to the front door. "It was cool but for the record please don't ever call me Daddy again. Only my

Queen and my kids are allowed to call me that. Oh yeah I left a little something for your mother on the table." With that he was out the door on his way home to handcuff Divine to the stove.

Trish stood in the middle of her living room floor feeling like shit. How the hell could he have her suck his dick then have the audacity to tell her never to call him Daddy? Then on top of that leave her mother two dime bags of heroin as if that was her payment for her sucking his dick. But that was okay she had something in store for Promise Dontae Green aka Rico.

SEVENTEEN

Divine was so happy that her eye had finally healed and she was able to get out of the house. Two weeks in the house without her children was enough to drive her crazy. And two weeks in the house with Promise expecting her to cook breakfast, lunch, and dinner was insane. He acted like her making him a quick meal was going to kill him. She could complain all she wanted but she did enjoy them having the house to themselves. Serving her King was something she enjoyed doing but never really had the time. Their children and the streets took up most of that.

Her first stop when she left the house was to Innocence house to spend time with her babies. She spent a good two hours there playing with both children but hated when it was time for her to leave and she could only take one child with her. She had promised Jamal that she would bring Knowledge to visit him and his family but Promise had made it perfectly clear that he didn't want Treasure to go along with them. It was one thing to confuse his son but he be damned if Divine had his daughter confuse in the process also. He didn't want Treasure believing that she had two daddies like her brother.

Divine couldn't believe how well Knowledge took to Jamal. It was like he has known him all of his two years of life that Promise wasn't his biological father. Jamal had planned an entire day with his son. They went out to eat, went to the movies, went clothes and toy shopping, and even did a couple of hours at Dave and Busters playing games. After their busy day he took his son and Divine to meet his grandmother. Divine absolutely adored Knowledge's great grandmother. She was the true representation of what was considered to be Big Mama. The entire time they were there the woman sat in the kitchen watching TV with Knowledge on her lap. This very well surprised Divine because her son didn't like to be held. He was the type of baby that liked to move around a lot by himself.

While Knowledge bonded with his great grandmother in the kitchen Divine did some bonding with Jamal in the finished attic. They talked about everything under the sun. She couldn't believe how open and honest she was being with him. She was more open with him about her feelings than she was with Promise. They must have run out of things to talk about because the next thing she knew Jamal's tongue was down her throat. She couldn't believe that they were kissing. Kissing wasn't one of her favorite past times and Promise's lips were the only lips that hers has ever touched. Now here was Jamal smothering her with his big juicy lips that for some reason they seemed to be the perfect match for hers. The way he snaked his tongue around hers was driving her insane.

She placed her hands on his chest, "Wait Jamal I can't do this. This is so fucking wrong."

He wasn't hearing nothing she was trying to say because he pushed her hands off his chest grabbed her head and proceeded to kiss her deeper than he was before.

This time she didn't attempt to push him away she jumped up off of the couch that they were sitting on. "For real Mal I can't do this."

He stood up in front of her. "Why can't you?"

"You know why. So let me grab my son and get the fuck outta here." She replied as she attempted to turn and walk down the stairs.

He grabbed her arm, "You mean my son and I think him spending the night with me wouldn't be such a bad idea."

Divine looked at him now knowing he was really crazy, "No it wouldn't be a bad idea, it would be a horrible idea. Today was his first day being around you that don't make him ready to spend the night away from his family."

"See that's what you keep forgetting, we are his family over here. You had him tucked away from me for the past two years and now you're telling me I can't get one night with my fuckin' son."

"That's not what I'm saying Jamal. You need to be understanding that he is only two years old and he has to get use to you and your family. Once that happens I would be more than glad to set up some arrangements for him to spend some nights. We can even alternate holidays if that's something you would like to do. But right now he needs to be phased in with your family. Please tell me you understand what I'm saying?"

"Yeah I understand what you're saying but that's not the real reason why he can't stay the night. You afraid Promise might knock your head off if you don't walk through the door with Knowledge. But seeing as though I'm a very understanding guy I'll let you have this fake ass phasing in process. Now gone downstairs and get my son and take him home it's getting late. I don't want you getting your ass whooped on my account."

Divine drove home so upset that she allowed Jamal to kiss her and even more upset that she enjoyed it. She really didn't understand where the kissing action came from because they didn't even kiss when they were a so called couple in high school. And she was even more upset that he called her on her bullshit lie about leaving her son with him overnight. If she would have come home without Knowledge Promise would have truly went upside her head and she honestly wasn't looking forward to that ever happening again. Some could say she was a sucka but after that ass whooping he gave her she would always play by his set of rules when it came to his son.

"Don't leave my son alone with that nigga, it's too fuckin' soon for all of that shit." His voice echoed through her ears. Yep she would play by his rules.

When she arrived home with Knowledge Promise was sitting on the couch with Treasure in his arms awaiting their arrival. And her poor daughter looked as if she was going to pass out from being so tired but once she saw her brother she jumped off the couch and ran to greet him.

"What she wouldn't go to sleep without her brother being here?"

"Man you already know."

After their brief encounter Promise left Divine alone with the children leaving her to be the one to tuck them in the bed for the night.

The moment she stepped through their bedroom door Promise was on her.

"I see the guilt written all over your face Doll. Now tell me what the fuck have you done."

"I haven't done anything Don damn. Whenever I leave the house now you find something to argue about when I come back home."

"Nice try. I keep telling you over and over again I know you better than you know yourself, now what are you feeling guilty about."

"Okay if you must know the truth the only thing I'm feeling guilty about is keeping Knowledge away from his family. Letting you name him as if he was rightfully yours without even consulting with his biological father. I mean for real Don I was wrong. I can see if the nigga wasn't shit yeah I wouldn't feel bad about what I did but the truth is he's a good dude and I robbed him and his family of two years of his son's life. Right is right and wrong is wrong and baby I was dead wrong. And they way Knowledge cried when I took him away from his great grandmother tore me apart. You and I both know that little boy don't cry for nothing, not even for us."

She walked away from Promise feeling like shit. Even though she started out lying to him about why she was feeling guilty but once she began to speak she did realize how wrong she was for playing with her son's life the way that she had. Not that she would ever take back how Promise and his family felt about her son embracing him as their own but seeing Knowledge interact with his blood family seemed so genuine.

She went into the bathroom to take her a hot bubble bath and attempt to soak away some of her wrong doing. She knew not to dare attempt to start washing herself up because Promise would swear up and down she was trying to wash away a nigga's nut. After sitting in the tub for about fifteen minutes she started to wonder where he was. She wasn't in the mood to holla his name so she sent him a quick text.

Me: I'm waiting

Don: Gone head, I'm cool

From his response she knew something was wrong. No matter what Promise never missed a chance to wash his heaven.

Me: Please, I'm too tired. I don't even know what to do because you bathe me all the time ;-)

Instead of responding to her text he stepped into the bathroom. And that's when she saw it, he had been crying. Now that was one thing her son had in common with Promise, never crying. She had known him since he was ten years old and she had never seen him drop a tear. Not once. Before he could even make it to the tub she had hopped out walked towards him dripping wet to embrace him with a hug.

"Oh my God Baby I am so sorry. Please tell me what I did wrong."

He wrapped his arms around her giving her his all. "Man you said that shit like I'm not his father. Like the love I have for him doesn't mean shit to you just because you grew some fuckin' balls and decided to tell the truth all of a sudden." He breathed heavily in the crook of her neck, "Man I would lay down my life for that little dude. Do you fuckin' understand that? I mean literally lay down my life. So don't you ever come in this house speaking to me about my son like that especially when you're covering up for something else. Do you understand me Divine Nanette?"

If she didn't hate herself before she hated herself now. Making Promise shed a tear because of her own guilt was something she wasn't going to forgive herself for anytime soon.

She hugged him even tighter because once again she was dead wrong. "I understand Don."

EIGHTEEN

Innocence mind had been all over the place for the past couple of weeks now. Seeing Promise's father after so many uncertain years had flooded her mind with a thousand memories. The one thing that was truly on her mind was has her son harmed his father. He had hardly spoken a word to her about the guy she saw walking down the street that day. She guessed her facial expression said all the words that her mouth couldn't.

Since her grandbabies had finally gone home she could now take a chance to see him again by herself. She hopped in her car to take a long drive finding every reason to drive down 146th street. Normally she didn't venture near the main part of Kinsman. She would usually get in her car and go in the opposite direction. She wasn't a fool she knew that was where her son did all of his dirty work so she always stayed away.

After driving around aimlessly for two hours she decided to give up and go home. She figured she would try to catch a glimpse of her son's father another day.

Cherokee sat under the hair dryer at Beauty Begins hair salon flipping through the latest issue of Essence magazine. They were featuring an article on couples getting the spark back in their relationships. Looking up from the magazine she noticed a familiar face walking through the shop doors. It was one of the many females that claim Sincere has the biggest dick on the planet. This female in particular was the one claiming she never had to worry about her rent being paid as long as Sincere kept raining tips on her. Watching the female's movement around the shop and thinking of the article she had just finished reading she realized what went wrong with her and Sincere's relationship.

Sincere love freaks and freaky shit. He was like the character from the Dr. Seuss book after he tasted the green eggs and ham. He wanted sex in a boat, with a goat, in the rain, on a train, in a box, with a fox, in a house, with a mouse, bottom line was Sincere loved spontaneous pussy and he wanted it any and everywhere but lately the only place he was getting it from Cherokee was at home in their bedroom. And surely that was not them. Now she knew exactly what to do to get his focus back on her. With her hair looking flawless with the layered body wrap she made her way to the nail shop to get a manicure and a pedicure. Her next stop was to the Fredrick lingerie shop. With everything on her agenda taken care of she headed home to put her plan in motion.

After hours of preparing herself for the nights events Cherokee stepped out knowing exactly where to find Sincere on a Friday night.

Sincere took his eyes off Sensual once he saw the female walking up the VIP stairs that has caught everyone's attention. A broad smile spread across his face as she reached the top of the stairs and he saw it was his Kee Baby that had all the niggas drooling.

He watched as she sashayed over wearing a mid-thigh trench coat tied securely around her waist, with some thigh high sheer stockings covering her slender legs, and with a pair of stilettos pumps on her small feet. He didn't know what she was wearing underneath but he was praying it was nothing. She walked up to the big booty female that came into the beauty salon earlier that day and whispered in her ear, "How much do you charge?"

"Twenty dollars a song"

Cherokee smiled as she placed a hundred dollar bill in the females garter belt, "I guess I have you the next five songs then. But no touching please, I only want to sit back and enjoy the sensual experience that I hear so much about." She then took her place on Sincere's lap to enjoy the show.

Sincere rubbed his hands up and down her thigh telling her how sexy she looked. Never speaking a word to him she discreetly unbuckled his pants then buried his pole deep inside of her. To the naked eye it looked as if she was simply sitting comfortably on his lap. As she kept eye contact with Sensual she slow grinded her pussy on Sincere's dick.

Whispering in her ear, "Kee Baby I swear I love the fuck out of you."

She looked back at him giving him the sexy smile she knew drove him crazy, "I know you do."

After two songs of slow grinding her pussy around on his dick she felt his manhood swell and explode inside of her. Not moving until she knew he had released every drop she eased a cloth out of her pocket then passed it to him letting him clean them so no one would notice. Once she was satisfied with his handy work and knowing his dick was securely tucked away in his pants she politely retrieved the cloth from him and placed it back in her coat pocket. She stood up from his lap and walked over to Sensual.

"He still has you for three more songs. And make it good please because what I seen I wasn't too impressed."

With that she left out of Tops and Bottoms with a smile on her face.

She wasn't comfortable in bed for more than fifteen minutes before she felt Sincere's body weight on top of her.

"What was that stunt you pulled tonight?" He asked as he slipped his dick inside of her.

She wrapped her arms around his neck and her legs around his waist, "Me playing my position."

He dug his dick deep inside of her, "And that's exactly why you're my star player."

After an hour of him bringing her body many orgasms she fell asleep with a smile on her face, *"Mission accomplished."*

NINETEEN

Promise sat on the edge of the bed watching Divine sleep. He admired her facial features as he stared down upon her. She looked so beautiful and peaceful as she slept. As he watched her he wondered to himself why in the hell did he cheat on her. He had no reasons. Yes he loved for women to need him but if he was ever in a serious bind would those same women be able to be there for him like his Doll would. Yes he also loved to see women walk around the house half naked everyday but most of his flings could afford to do that because they didn't have children running around their house. He could honestly admit that whenever his babies were away from the house his Queen would always have on something sexy that would catch his eye. He really loved the days when she would walk around the house cleaning, cooking, and doing laundry without anything on but a pair of heels. Now that shit right there drove him insane. He smiled to himself thinking, *damn I love this woman.*

He slid into bed behind her pulling her close to him. He then whispered in her ear, "Doll I don't know why I do half the shit I do but I promise you from this day on I'm going to tighten my shit up. Those broads in the streets aren't worth my home life."

She snuggled up even closer to him, "Actions speaks louder than words" and then she drifted back off to sleep.

Promise shifted in his sleep once he felt Divine moving to get out of bed. He grabbed her pulling her back to him, "Where do you think you're going?"

"To use the bathroom"

He loosened his grip then instructed her to hurry back.

When she got back in the bed he pulled her into his arms. He then rested his hand on her lower abdomen. He caressed her stomach softly. "When are you going to bless me Doll?

She sighed. The only thing that he has been focused on lately was getting her pregnant. Did he care that they already had two, two year olds running around their house? Did he care that they both were still in the streets already not spending enough time with the two they had? Did he care that their relationship was so fucked up at times? Wasn't he the very one claiming he didn't know why he couldn't keep his dick to himself just a few hours ago?

"Do you want me to be honest with you Don?"

She felt his hand tense on her stomach.

"Speak Divine."

"See right now when I asked you do you want me to be honest your body tensed up getting ready for war. Baby I swear sometimes I don't understand this neurotic behavior you have for me. I used to think it was cute to have someone gone over me and would do anything for me. But now I see that shit is crazy. Baby you're so gone that bodies have went six feet under and I don't want to even mention the ass whoopin' you gave me all because you can't control yourself. So I'm going to say this, when you can show me it's all about me and our family without all the aggressiveness and possessiveness, when you learn to control that crazy ass Aries temper of yours, and when your dick is mine and I mean all mine, then I will bless you. I promise."

He kissed the back of her neck, "Get my temper and dick in check. I can handle that."

She turned to face him, "I know you can Daddy."

She slid her arm around him and began to gently rub his back. She then paraded soft kisses on his chest.

Right when he was about to move his hand down to his heaven his phone began to vibrate on the night stand. He tried to ignore it put the caller was being very persistent. Realizing they weren't going to stop calling he went ahead and answered the call.

"This better be life or death."

Pops chuckled on the other end of the phone, "I won't say life or death but what I want to discuss is kind of urgent."

"I'll be there in about an hour." Promise mumbled in the phone knowing it was serious because Pops never dialed his number. Divine was his favorite contact person.

He tried to resume where he left off at with his hand headed towards his heaven but she stopped him in his tracks.

"Go see about Pops, your heaven isn't going anywhere."

"How did you know it was him on the phone?"

"I heard his voice. You keep your volume so high on your phone its ridiculous. So just to let you know I hear a lot of your conversations when you're in ear shot. You need to keep that in mind."

He kissed her on her forehead, "I already told you don't have to worry about any of that anymore."

"I hear you talking Don, now go handle that and hurry back home."

"Yes Mommy!"

Before Promise could knock on the door good Pops swung it open. "We have a slight problem and I do mean slight."

Promise took off his jacket and laid it across the arm of the sofa. "What problem may that be?"

"Your damn sister, I put her on Barns you put her on Barns and I'll be damned if this damn girl done fell in love. And when I say in love I mean in love." Pops vented as he paced his living room floor. "I mean it really isn't a big issue for me because I'm still going to do the dirty cat but I don't want Diamond losing her mind when the dope fiend comes up missing. I mean this girl came over here today begging and pleading for the man's life like he's not the enemy."

Promise groaned. "It don't matter Pops she's just going to have to deal with it and if she can't all I can say is jail is not an option. So take that how you want. That's why I think we should make sure he get his hands on something a little too strong for his system, making him overdose. She can't argue too much with that."

"I figured that was what you wanted to do. You're always the diplomatic one wanting everything to blow over smoothly. But what I had in store for his crooked ass all of the cops will think twice before they fuck with me and mines again."

Now Pops really had Promise intrigued. He leaned forward with his eyebrow raised on his forehead, "What do you have in mind old man?"

TWENTY

Divine awoke in the middle of the night only to find that Promise hasn't come back home. She wouldn't have gave to much thought to it thinking he probably was taking care of business but knowing him he would have called or texted and said that. She figured she wasn't going to read too far into it seeing as though he might have forgotten to call, so she decided to call him. After her calling his phone a good five times and getting no answer she really began to worry. One thing Promise didn't do was not answer her phone calls. If he was angry with her he would pick up his phone to let her know he was cool then would hang up in her face. Even if he was laid up with a female he would still answer her phone call. So it was safe to say she was worried about her King.

Her first phone call was to Pops to see if everything went good with them and if Promise left his house in one piece. He assured her that everything was cool and that Promise told him he was on his way home to lie back down.

Her second call was to Innocence house to see if he stopped by there. Innocence told her that she had talked to him early but hasn't seen him all day.

Her third call was to Sincere. She figured that the two haven't spent a lot of time together lately so maybe they hooked up doing God knows what. He answered the phone all groggy letting her know he was knocked out and haven't even seen Promise all week.

Now her spidey senses was really all over the place. And for some reason she knew he wasn't sitting in anyone's jail cell. She decided to do something that she promised herself she would never do. And the only reason she was going to do it this time was because the clown was just in their bed telling her he was going to keep his dick to himself. She called Innocence back to see if she would come and sit with the kids while she went to see if she could find Promise, which Innocence had no problem with cause now she was worried herself wondering if her son was okay especially if Divine couldn't get a hold of him.

The moment Innocence stepped through her door Divine was stepping out heading to the Westside.

Just as Divine thought, there was her man's truck sitting in his bitch's Trish driveway. Sitting across the street from the house she dialed his number again only to receive no answer. She was so upset with him she didn't know what to do. Maybe she should play crazy like he do and burst in the girl's house and drag him out by his beard. But nawl that wasn't her style. If that's where he wanted to lay his head for the night then so be it.

As she pulled away from the curb an eerie feeling came over her. Something just wasn't right about the situation. Promise not answering his phone was really starting to get to her. Even though Promise played with a lot of females in the streets she always came first.

She have drove halfway home before deciding to turn her car around.

Before getting out of her car she made sure her trusty 9mm was snuggled on her hip then she politely walked up to the door and began to ring the doorbell. She could here movement on the other side of the door so she knew Trish was looking out of the peep hole at her.

Trish stared out of the peep hole shocked. All she kept saying to herself was, *"What the fuck? No his bitch isn't at my door at three o'clock in the morning, I can't fuckin' believe this shit. And here I was thinking that I was the insecure one in this love triangle."*

Mustering up enough nerve she finally decided to answer her door.

"Um, who is it?"

"Doll"

"Doll who?"

Divine rolled her eyes in the top of her head, "You know exactly who I am just like I know who you are so could you please tell Rico I'm at the door."

Her calling Promise by the name Rico really had Trish furious. Not only did his bitch know about her and where she lived she also knew the fake ass name that he had told her also. Now she really wasn't mad about what she had done to him.

"You right I do know who you are but I'm sorry to inform that Rico is sleeping right now and he told me not to disturb him. Not trying to be funny or nothing but you have been calling his phone for the past hour and he haven't answered so doesn't that kind of tell you something?"

Divine did everything that she could to hold her composure on the other side of the door because she knew the broad was staring at her through the peep hole. So being the woman that she was she bowed out gracefully telling Trish that she was absolutely right and to inform Rico that she came by looking for him.

Trish damn near jumped for joy when Divine left off her porch and went in got in her car. She couldn't believe how well Promise had his Queen trained. Figured she got rid of Divine she went back to work on Promise.

Divine drove her car one block over then put in a call to the Fam.

"What's good big Sis?" Dre asked answering his phone sounding half dead.

She explained to him in as much code as she could that she needed a cleanup team at Promise's Westside bitch house because she was about to murder the hoe.

After placing her phone call she reached in her glove comportment to retrieve her tight fitting leather gloves and a set of house keys.

See what Promise other females didn't realize was that if they kept dope in their house for him then that meant Divine had a key. But why wouldn't she, it was also her dope and most of the females he fucked with only just served as a place to store it. She guessed Trish would be very upset if she'd known that Divine has been in her house on numerous occasions storing dope.

She walked back around the corner towards the house. She eased around to the back door unlocking the door very quietly. She tiptoed up the stairs to the master bedroom figuring that had to be the room they would be in at three thirty in the morning.

When she opened the bedroom door she got the biggest shock of her life.

She raised her gun at Trish, "Bitch what the fuck did you do to him?"

The moment those words left her lips she heard Dre and his goons busting through the door. "Man what the fuck?" were Promise's little brother exact words.

Divine tucked her gun in the waist of her pants and rushed over to Promise as she barked orders. "I swear don't nobody let this bitch out of their sight. Tie her ass up and I mean right now."

Whatever sweet revenge smile Trish had on her face faded away once Divine startled her with her gun pointing at her. Then when all the niggas filled the room with their guns locked and loaded she pissed on herself then fell to the floor.

Divine kneeled down by the side of the bed where Promise was knocked out. She gently withdrew the needle that was hanging out of his arm and untied the tourniquet. She slapped him on his face trying to get him to wake up but he wasn't responding. She continued to slap him and call his name but he was too zoned out. She screamed across the room in the direction where Trish was in the process of being tied up, "How much did you fucking give him you stupid bitch?"

Trish sobbed and sobbed.

"Bitch I said how much?"

Dre walked over to Trish and back handed her, "Bitch fucking answer her!"

Divine knew it was useless to get the broad to talk because her facial expression looked like she was scared as hell, like she knew she was about to lose her life which she was.

"Get that dumb hoe out of here now!"

She turned her attention back to Promise. She put her ear near his mouth and nose to see if he was still breathing only to find that his breaths were very faint. She knew in a moment his body might shut down.

Right when she was about to bark the next order for someone to go in the bathroom and turn on the shower water Sincere busted in the room.

Instantly he jumped into motion. He went over to the bed where five of them picked Promise up and took him to the shower.

By the time they got him to the shower Divine was already sitting in the tub under the cold running water telling them to hurry up.

She held Promise in her arms under the freezing cold water begging him not to fucking die on her. She did everything from smacking him to pulling on his earlobes to kissing his discolored lips.

She looked up at Sincere only to see him standing there motionless with tears running down his face.

She screamed to the top of her lungs, **"Sincere please do something, I can't fuckin' lose him!"**

TWENTY ONE

Sincere snapped out of his trance and walked over to Dre. He told him to get rid of the broad and to clear all the dope out of the house. He then instructed the strongest men that they had so they could lift Promise out of the tub and take him out to the truck. He gave Dre his car keys along with Divine's so he could get their cars out of sight. He grabbed Divine out of the tub and carried her in his arms as he walked behind the goons that were carrying Promise. After he got them situated in the trucks back seat he hopped in the driver's seat headed to Metro hospital.

Divine held Promise's head in her lap praying that he didn't overdose on her. She rubbed and admired ever feature on his face wondering what the hell happen between him and the broad to make her want to drug him like she did. All she could think of was that the female wanted more from him that he wasn't willing to give. No matter what female he entertained in the streets his heart will always belong to her and he is very honest about it with his flings.

She bent down to whisper in his ear, "Don I know you can beat this. Out of all the ways you could die please don't let this be one of them. Please baby." She then gave a slight chuckle, "I don't even know why I'm trippin'. You die and leave me, in yo dreams nigga. You probably got the devil collared up right now telling him it ain't your time. As a matter of fact I know that's exactly what you're doing. So hang on just a little while longer we're almost at the hospital."

Promise eyes shifted behind his eyelids. He could hear faint voices talking and could hear a lot of beeping sounds. From all of the sounds around him he came to the conclusion that he was in the hospital. He tried to open his eyes but they wouldn't budge.

He listened closely to the voices around him and knew that one of them belonged to his beautiful Queen. He could faintly remember her beating and crying over him begging him not to die. He smiled knowing she was there for him and thinking to himself not in a million years would he leave her.

He couldn't wait until he could finally wake from whatever zone he was in so he could let her know what had happened and how he ended up over Trish's house in the first place.

Pops arrived at the hospital even after Divine had called to let him know Promise was okay. He had to make sure with his own two eyes. He stood in the corner of the waiting area thinking how different him and his son's relationship would have been if he would have told him sooner. He wondered how Innocence would have reacted to him showing up at her door steps over twenty years ago. His mind was disrupted of its wondering when he saw Innocence coming through the waiting room doors. He quickly turned not wanting her to see his face. He could hear her talking to Sincere asking what had happened to her son. To his surprise she took the news very well. He thought she would be crying her eyes out screaming and shouting about her son. He was happy to know that she was strong now. She wasn't little Ms. Innocence Green, green to the game anymore.

He couldn't hear her talking anymore so he peeped over his shoulder to see if she had left out of the waiting room. But to his surprise she was looking directly at him. He instantly turned to walk out of the room guessing he would see about his son at another time. By the time he made to the door entrance he felt a hand on his arm.

"Sincere tells me that your name is Pops but I got a feeling that's just a name they call you, so don't you think it's about time you and I have a proper introduction?"

Pops turned to come face to face with the beautiful woman that he raped, tortured, and fell in love with twenty two years ago. "It's Samuel Carter."

She held out her delicate hand, "It's nice to finally meet you Samuel Carter."

He took her hand inside of his, "Is it possible for us to go somewhere and talk?"

"Lead the way," she replied giving him a slight smile.

They ventured to an empty family waiting room. Innocence politely sat on the couch crossing her legs like the girlie girl that she was. Pops couldn't help but admire the beautiful woman that she has grown to be. He watched her over the past twenty years becoming more intrigued by her every day. Everything about the woman was sexy. The fact that she was strong enough to put up with her husband's shit was one of them. Then her physical attributes he didn't even know where to begin with them. Maybe he would start with her long lean body that only the females from the reality show America's Next Top Model possessed. Or with her smooth light skin that looks as if she was dipped in a big bowl of vanilla ice cream. No he knew where he should start, with the first thing someone would fall in love with the moment they would lay eyes on her. Her beautiful oval shaped face that housed the perfect pair of dark penetrating eyes, a small button nose, and with a pair of sexy thin lips that yearned to be kissed.

"Um Samuel you said you wanted to talk but all you're doing is staring."

He snapped out of his trance and took a seat next to her.

"I really don't know where to begin but I guess I'm sorry would be a start. Innocence I am so sorry for what I did to you those years back. I was a different man living in a different time. I mean you have to understand that it wasn't my intentions to hurt you the way I did, but that was my world. Your dude disrespected me by stealing from me so I had no choice. But I ……"

She silenced him by putting her finger up to his lips. "That was over twenty years ago, I can honestly say you have redeemed yourself over the years. You gave me a handsome son that you help me raise financially over the years. Well let's say you helped me raise all my children financially. You made sure me and my children wanted for nothing. And I guess I should thank you for that. How we were thrown together those years ago was crazy but I can say I don't regret one thing I endured while I was held captive in your home. All we can do now is move forward. Our son knows the truth and for you to be sitting here now lets me know that he has accepted whatever place you have in his life. So now all we have to do is worry about him." She shook her head slowly, "I don't even know what happened to my baby and it's scaring the shit out of me."

He took her hand inside his again and explained to her what Sincere had explained to him assuring her that their son was going to be okay. Then he remembered something. "Innocence where are the grandbabies? From my understanding they were with you."

She nonchalantly waved her hand, "I dropped them off to my house with my youngest daughter Destiny. Thanks for being concerned though."

He cupped her chin turning her face towards him, "Haven't you realized by now that I have always been concerned?"

TWENTY TWO

After being out of it for days it seemed like Promise finally opened his eyes. He adjusted his sight to the darkened room to see he was alone except for the extra body heat he was starting to feel. He looked down and of course his Queen was snuggled up against him on the hospital bed sleeping soundly. He gently massaged her cheek. She smiled in her sleep. He rubbed his fingers through her short cropped hair. She stirred in her sleep a little. He then cupped her chin tilting her face up towards him then placed a soft kiss on her forehead. This time she tightened her body against his and smiled up at him without opening her eyes.

"How do you feel Daddy?"

"As good as I can feel after almost overdosing." He responded as he still rubbed his fingers gently on her cheek.

Snuggling closer to him, "You want to tell me what happened now or later when you're comfortable at home?"

"Now is cool but first tell me is the bitch dead?"

"Not yet."

He lifted her head off his chest and looked at her with a confused expression on his face, "Why not?"

"Because I want to kill your whore myself and I couldn't do that while I was at the hospital waiting to see what was going on with you. But trust me Don soon as you get out of here she's the first thing on my agenda.

And before you ask yes everything was cleaned out of her house. Even her shit."

He smiled down at her, "That's my girl. Well to make a long story short about how I got over there, she texted me saying she thought someone has been in her house because the basement door was open. As you and I both know I was concerned because that's where the safe was that housed the dope. So I made my way over there after I hollered at Pops. Once I got there I checked the safe and everything seemed to be okay so then she asked can she holla at me about some real shit. I went to her refrigerator to pour me a cup of Kool-Aid then went to her bedroom because that's where she was. All I know is that I sat down on her bed drinking the Kool-Aid and listening to her talk then everything went blank. After that all I heard was you begging me not to die on you. I felt us under the cold shower, I felt you kissing my lips, I felt them putting me in the truck, and I felt when they started hooking me up to shit in this hospital. From all of that I know for sure that she had something in that damn Kool-Aid." He stopped talking so he could scratch his inside of his arm. "Doll you have to believe me, I did not go over there to fuck that girl after I told you that I was going to keep my dick to myself. I know that's what you were thinking."

"That's what I thought at first Baby but once I seen you passed out with that damn needle in your arm I didn't care if you fucked her mama. All I wanted was for you to survive."

She took her hand and laid it on top of his where he was scratching his arm. "Do you think this is going to be a problem?"

He stopped scratching, "I swear to God I hope not Doll, but if I feel any temptations you know you will be the first person I come to."

"I know Don."

"This some karma for my ass huh?"

Giving a slight chuckle Divine replied, "Yeah I guess you can say that."

"How is my mother doing? I know she was worried out of her mind."

"That she was her and Pops. They both were here last night."

She could feel his body tensing up after her last statement.

"Did that nigga touch my mother Doll?"

"Relax Baby, no he did not. Actually they had a long talk about their situation."

"Doll I don't want that fuckin' rapist around my mother."

She inhaled deeply, "Baby that's not my choice nor is it yours. Innocence seems to be comfortable around him so we're going to leave it at that. If you would for one moment think of their situation and how they were thrown into it maybe you would be more understanding. You're so angry at Pops when all your frustrations should be on Big Dee. Don think about our lifestyle. If the situation would have happened to you, no you wouldn't have held her hostage waiting for him to pay his debt you would have killed the innocent female on the spot. I know it's fucked up what happened between them but they have seemed to have gotten over it and in some way I think they fell in love with each other those years back. Think about it Don that man took care of you and your family over the years and your mother allowed him to. She didn't have to live in that house and she damn sure didn't have to accept his money. In some way I think she was waiting on him to return."

"Yeah you might be right Doll but if I see anything going wrong with my mother it won't be anything you can say to keep me off Pops ass."

She reached up and kissed his dry lips, "Don if he put some bullshit in the game I would be more than happy to sit by and watch whatever you have in store for him."

For the rest of the night they talked about everything under the sun not closing their eyes once. Promise was so happy when the doctor came in that morning and gave him a clean bill of health for him to go home. All he wanted to do was go home and lay around the house spending time with his babies. The only thing the two had to worry about now was if his body was going to be craving the heroin.

TWENTY THREE

Divine watched from the side line as Promise played with the children. She knew he loved his babies more than anything in the world so she figured she would give him a moment alone with them. She laughed as Knowledge showed him how to work the Kindle Fire so he could read a story to them. *The son teaching the father how to work technology WOW!* Knowledge was practically picture reading the book to his dad and sister. He recited the words he knew by heart "Zippity Nippity Nook, please take care of the book."

Promise felt Divine eyes on them. He glanced up at her and smiled, "This little boy is going to be a genius Doll."

"I agree. Baby I hate to break up y'all reading party but I have some good news and some bad news for you."

She saw his jaw twitch so she made her way over to the couch where they were sitting and sat down next to him. She intertwined her fingers with his. She has found that to be the most effective gesture to calm him.

He stared her in her eyes, "Give me the bad first."

"Well Baby I know you've going to be upset and all because you just came home from the hospital, but remember this is Jamal's weekend to have Knowledge. I tried to reschedule with him but he has already made reservations to take him to Kalahari."

"See Doll, this the bullshit I'm talking about. The nigga interfering with my time with my son, I'm not liking this shit one bit. And we just took him there last month. He don't need to go back so soon."

"Don he went with us as a family, now Jamal wants to take him so he could have some fun with him. He doesn't even know I took him last month. I don't volunteer any information about what we're doing over here."

"We," He responded cutting her off.

Looking confused, "What?"

"You said he doesn't know you took him last month when you should have said we took him last month." He sighed looking at her sideways. "What I'm really starting to have a problem with is you forgetting that that's my fuckin' son right there. Let me set the record straight right now, if I have to keep reminding you of that, that nigga is going to be six feet under just like your other supposed to be baby daddy. And if your ass got another mystery nigga up your sleeve I'm going to put your ass six feet under with all them niggas. Do you fuckin' understand me?"

She politely shook her head yes.

This time he thumbed her on the side of her head. "I have no idea of what that means. Now I asked you do you understand me?"

"Yes Don."

"What's the good news you got for me?"

"After I drop Knowledge off I'm going to handle that one situation."

He untwined his fingers from hers, "Drop Treasure off to Innocence on your way and hurry your ass back."

After getting everything squared away with Promise she ran up the stairs so she could jump in the shower. Once clean she threw on her I don't give a fuck clothes, an all-black Nike track suit with her all black ACG duck boots. Yep today was that day. She gathered her kids then headed out the front door.

She dialed Jamal's number knowing she was going to hear him fuss and that's exactly what he did as soon as he answered his phone.

"You should have been here over an hour ago Vines, what's up," Jamal spat into his cell without even saying so much as a hello to her.

"I know I'm running behind schedule but I had to drop my daughter off to her grandmother's house before I came."

"You couldn't have brought him first then dropped her off. That would have made more sense seeing as though I'm trying to be on the highway by a certain time."

She sat on the phone listening to him mumble getting angrier by the second. She was so tired of him and Promise getting on her back about her son, because at the end of the day that's what he was. Her fucking son!

"You know what Jamal, I'm not about to go through this with you. All I hear is you complaining and I have more important things I need to be doing right now. So the question is do you want me to drop him off or not? She asked seriously aggravated.

"Yeah bring him on." He responded then hanging up in her face.

She looked at the phone sideways. I'm so tired of these over aggressive ass niggas I don't know what to do. *My poor son is going be like a pit bull on steroids being raised by these two animals.* Still driving she promised herself she wasn't going to let Jamal upset the rest of her day. She had something very important to deal with and she needed to be focused.

Once she pulled in his driveway there he was of course looking mad as shit. She hopped out of the car then grabbed her son from the back seat. She handed Knowledge and his things to his dad making sure she gave Jamal I don't feel the fuck like it expression. She then addressed her attention towards her son.

"Now Boo-Man you be very good for your dad. I don't want him telling me you were a bad boy. You got that big man?"

"Yes Mommy."

"I know you do, now give your mommy a kiss so I can go."

Sincere rode up Chagrin Boulevard thinking about his cousin. He wondered how in the hell did Promise get so comfortable with a sideline female to almost have her take his life. He knew Promise fucked whatever female housed his dope but to him it had to be more to it than that. He figured his nigga had to be saying sweet nothings in the broads' ear for them to be falling all in love with him the way they do. It was never a mystery to anyone about Promise feelings towards Divine but for some reason the nigga had to have a hoe that needed him in one way or another. It was something he didn't quite understand. He himself loved the fact that when it was all said and done Cherokee didn't need him. She was with him because she loved him and would do anything for him the same as Divine was with Promise. But for some reason his cousin couldn't keep his dick out of a needy hoes pants.

Man I can't be passing judgment on nobody seeing as though my dick stay in a stripper's ass. He thought as he bust a left on Richmond Road heading to go holla at his little cousin.

Promise answered his door surprised to see Sincere standing there.

"Damn P, you go let a nigga in or what?"

"Nigga shut the fuck up and get yo' ass in here." Promise responded while hugging his favorite cousin in a bear hug.

As Sincere got comfortable on the couch he noticed there wasn't anyone else home.

"Where Doll and the kids at?"

"You just missed them. She took Treasure to Innocence and Knowledge to that nigga. After that she's going to handle that one piece of business."

"So how you dealing with the new baby daddy situation?"

"Man, I'm not. That nigga go be dead by the end of this year."

Sincere shook his head, "P you can't keep going around killing niggas because they got a small piece of my sis. Damn nigga."

"Says who?" Promise asked giving him the 'who gone do something about it' look on his face.

"It's yo world P. Anyway I'm glad she going to handle that other shit, hearing that hoe sob all day starting to get on my last nerves. And on that note I'm glad you came out of that bullshit okay. Nigga if you would have died, man I don't know what my sister would have done me either for that matter."

"I know right."

"For real though P, that shit would have been all bad seeing as though we ain't even kick it in a minute. I ain't on no gay shit but Cuz I miss the fuck out of you. All type of shit been going on in my world too and I ain't even got at my nigga to let him know what's up." Sincere stated as he pulled out a stick of weed from his top jacket pocket and pointed it in Promise's direction, "Blaze up my nigga!"

As Promise went on to light the weed Sincere took the opportunity to fill him in on what's been going on with his life. He informed him of the horrible night Cherokee had gotten raped and how fucked up he has been in the head ever since.

Promise interrupted his story because he had one question he needed answered. "Is the nigga dead?"

Sincere shook his head, "That's the thing she said she don't have any idea who the nigga was. Trust if she knew that muthafucka would have been dead the moment his name left her lips. And on that note, P this love shit is crazy. I know I got on your ass about being retarded about Doll but nigga I'm just as crazy about Kee ass. Nigga I been doing some ole sucka shit too, going through her phone, asking her daughter where they been, and my latest is following her around then calling her to see if she go lie about her whereabouts."

Promise started cracking up and choking of the weed at the same time.

"P this shit ain't funny for real. Shit I'm on the verge of saying fuck a relationship so I can keep my damn sanity."

Promise passed the blunt back to him, "Nigga shut up a smoke, yo' ass ain't going anywhere and you know it. You in love so chalk it up and take one for the team. But on the real you know I'm the last person you need to talking to about some in love shit cause you already know if I think shit ain't right between mine, and a nigga is involved, somebody go' be dead. No questions asked." He paused looking at Sincere with a serious look on his face, "On some real shit though Sin, no matter what y'all going through try not to put your hands on her. Y'all can talk, holla, scream, tear shit up in the house, just don't put your hands on her man. That shit alone will give you nightmares, knowing you hurt the most precious thing in your life."

Sincere gave him a skeptical look, "Nigga you put your hands on my sister or something?"

"That's a whole other conversation for another day."

Sincere sat up in the reclining chair to put the blunt out in the ashtray. "Nawl nigga today is always a good day, now nigga did you put your hands on my sister?"

Promise inhaled deeply and stared at his cousin. The last thing he wanted to do was have an all-out brawl in his house with his family about his bitch. He was about to do something he has never done because lying was never a part of his character. "Put my hands on Doll nigga fuck nawl. Nigga do you see any bullet holes in me? You know my Queen has no problem wit' pulling out her trusty sidekick?"

Sincere relaxed in his chair, "Nigga you had me scared for a minute."

The two enjoyed each other's company and a couple of more blunts for the next two hours before Sincere parted promising his cousin he would be back the next day to kick it with him.

TWENTY FOUR

Trish sat tied to a chair reeking of her own feces and urine. She didn't know how long she had been there but it felt like forever. She was praying that someone came to see about her soon. She felt at some point they were going to let her go because she was still alive. If they wanted her dead it would have happened by now, so she thought.

What she was really hoping for was for Promise to come talk to her so she could explain her actions because she wasn't by any means trying to kill him. If he gave her a chance to explain she could let him know how he hurt her that day he left the dope on the table for her mother after she sucked his dick like she wasn't shit. She would explain to him how much she has been in love with him all of her life and how she wanted him to herself. She would let him know how she was tired of competing with Divine for his love.

That's what she would try to express to him but her motives were totally different. What she really wanted to do was bring him down off of his throne and make him dependent on her. She knew Divine wouldn't accept him in her life with a drug habit. If he would at some point formed a habit for the heroin she herself would accept him with open arms because all she has ever wanted was for him to be a part of her life.

She could faintly here footsteps coming down the stairs so she looked up to the ceiling saying, "Finally, thank God."

"God-damn you stink" Divine spoke as she reached the bottom step.

"Where's Promise?"

"Promise? So you knew who he was all this time, huh?"

"Why wouldn't I know who he was, I've been in love with him my whole life. Now where the hell is he?" She spoke as if she had some type of authority in the situation.

Divine stood in front of her but kept her distance because she was stinking like a muthafucka. "Help me understand Trish, you drug the man you so call love almost killing him and now you're demanding to know where he is? Bitch is you retarded? What you need to be concerned about is your own fuckin' self, not worried about mine. And since you know Promise so well you know that's exactly who he is, mine."

Trish smacked her lips as if Divine standing in front of her with a gun didn't faze her at all.

Divine shook her head not believing the balls on this female. Did she honestly think Promise was concerned about her? She smiled at her as she took the silencer out of her track suit jacket pocket. "You know what, you claim to know Promise so well but yet you're sitting here so sure of your life. I don't get that.

Sometimes I wonder to myself where the fuck do my King get y'all retarded ass bitches from."

She raised her gun putting two silent slugs in Trish's head.

"I truly wonder sometimes," was the last thing she spoke as she walked away from Trish's dead body.

She skipped up the basement stairs closing the door behind her. She walked up to DeAndre who was sitting at the kitchen table weighing up some dope.

"Lil Bro, please get somebody to get rid of that funky ass body, like now."

"I got you Doll. So how is P doing?"

"He cool"

He looked up from what he was doing to ask her again because he didn't want any miscommunications, "No, I mean how is he doing?"

By the way he was looking at her she knew exactly what he was referring to. "For now he's cool. He doesn't get to much sleep though, a lot of tossing and turning but like I said for now."

"Yeah I feel you. Let him know I'll be up there to see about him once I take care of everything on this end."

After giving him a kiss on the forehead and assuring him she would relay the message she was out the door headed to the grocery store so she could prepare a feast for her King.

Once she arrived home with all the groceries Promise had let her know that she had just missed Sincere for all of five minutes.

She said a silent damn to herself as she started putting the groceries away because she would have loved to see her big brother. She never gave him the proper thanks for taking charge with getting Promise to the hospital.

Promise sat in a kitchen chair watching his Queen prepare their meal for the night figuring now would be the best time to let her know what has been going on with him.

"Doll I'm starting to feel real funny sometimes, especially at night."

She instantly stopped what she was doing and took in couple of deep breaths as her heart began to beat faster because she knew what he was referring to. Making her way over to him she straddled his lap and began to hug him tight kissing the crook of his neck, his cheek, and then his lips.

"How bad is it?"

"Not bad, just a feeling I've never felt before so I know where it's stemming from."

"Do you think it's time for us to seek some help?"

"Not yet Baby, I'm cool. If it gets worse trust me I'll let you know then we'll figure something out."

"You promise?"

He caressed her back and planted soft kisses on her neck. "I promise Doll."

They stayed hugged that way for the next couple of minutes with Divine silently wishing that she could bring that hoe Trish back to life so she could kill her ass all over again.

⁂

Sincere drove home with one thing on his mind, being between Cherokee's petite legs. But once he pulled in his driveway he got a rude awakening because her car wasn't anywhere in sight. He immediately picked up his phone and dialed her number.

"Yes Babe," she answered with a smile plastered across her face.

"Where the fuck you at?"

She looked at her cell confused, "Well right now I'm driving home and why are you talking to me like that. What's wrong?"

"I'm home and you're not. That's what's wrong, now get here." He barked then hung up in her face.

By the time she pulled up to the house he was already waiting for her in the doorway with an angry look on his face. She didn't waist anytime locking up her car and hurrying in the house. When she stepped all the way through the front door it slammed behind her with her being pushed up against it.

"Where you been Kee?" He asked her as he pressed his body against hers and roamed his hands all over her body.

"I went to drop Shereé off at her grandma Jackie's house," she gasped as she felt his hands slide down the front of her pants to her pussy.

He played with her sticky core for a couple of seconds before asking, "Then why the fuck is your pussy so wet if that was all you were doing?"

She grabbed a hold of his shoulders because she was definitely on the verge of cumming. "Babe it's wet because of you."

"Nawl come better than that Kee, you just walked through the door. It shouldn't be dripping like this."

"Sincere I think I creamed my panties the moment you threw my back against the door." She squealed as he began to circle her clit.

He pressed his mouth against her ear breathing heavily inside, "You telling me you like it when I give it to you rough like this?" Asking as he tore open her jeans and slid them to the floor pulling her soaking wet panties to the side then smothering his face in her pussy.

"Oh God yes Sincere…"

He took a moment's pause to look up at her, "Oh God yes Sincere what?"

Staring back down at him she rubbed his handsome face. "I more than like it when you give it to me like this Baby, I love it."

With that he stood up from his squatting position picked her up and carried her up the stairs to their bedroom. He threw her on the bed pulling off her panty and jeans completely. Getting down on his knees he wrapped her legs around his forearms then pulled her towards him with much force making her body bounce on the bed. He spread her legs wide so he could get a good view of her pussy. What he saw before him was a lovely sight. Her pussy was so pretty it had him salivating at the mouth. Putting his mouth as close as he could to her beautiful core without touching he inhaled her arousal.

"Whose pussy is this Kee?"

Feeling his hot breath on her was enough to make her cum in itself. She couldn't possibly fathom what it was about him to make her love him the way she does, but whatever it was she was never letting him go.

"It's yours Sin."

He looked up at her with sadness in his eyes, "Promise me you will never let another man come near you. If someone tries to ever violate you again promise me you will shoot him dead between the eyes for trying to fuck with mines."

She stared down at him knowing what had happened to her hurt him more than it did her. And no she wouldn't let another man touch her again. She will kill or die trying to keep what belongs to Sincere safe.

"I promise Baby."

Once those words left her lips she felt him twirling his tongue around her clit. *Damn he didn't waste any time,* she thought.

After making her cum more than once in his mouth he penetrated her tight walls slowly, easing in inch by inch. Biting her bottom lip she looked up at him with pure ecstasy written all over her face. He knew she wanted it rough but he missed her insides so much he wanted to fill her every nook and cranny with his slow whine.

"Damn I missed this pussy Kee." He whispered in her ear as he dug deep inside her.

She hugged him around his neck tightly as she wrapped her legs around his waist then grinding her pussy back at him.

"This pussy misses you too Baby but I miss us. I want us back Sin," She spoke while moaning in his ear.

"You got that." He responded now picking up his pace.

"Oh yes Sincere…"

He could feel her insides beginning to tighten around his dick. She was trying to fight it, trying to hold out but he wasn't having it. He hasn't felt her cum on his dick in weeks.

Biting her right shoulder he moaned in her ear, "Don't play with me Kee, give it to me baby." He dug deeper. "Damn this pussy feel good. You say it's mine now give it to me."

She couldn't hold back any more, "Yes… Oh God… Sincere here it comes… Damn baby, I'm cumming…"

"That's what the fuck I'm talking about Kee, cum on this dick."

He grinded his dick in and out of her at a rapid pace knowing she would be cumming again in a matter of seconds and he be damned if he wasn't going to be cumming along with her.

"Oh my God… Yes Sin, right there baby… I'm cumming baby, shit, shit, shit."

"That's right cum on this dick." He groaned as he came along with her shooting his hot seed deep inside.

Catching his breath he rolled off of her pulling her on top of him gently rubbing his hand up and down the spin of her back.

"I mean what the fuck I said Kee. Shoot that muthafucka dead between the eyes."

"Yes Sincere."

TWENTY FIVE

Pops had been spending a lot of time on the phone talking with Innocence ever since that night at the hospital. She wanted so desperately to see him face to face and spend time with him but he wasn't ready for that. He would love to interact with her and the grandbabies but he wasn't going to make that move without Promise's consent. Even though he and his son still had a relationship he didn't think Promise would approve of him having one with his mother. And he could truly understand why not. He had raped the most precious female on earth which was Promise's mother and there wasn't any way around that. All he could do now is prove to his only son that he was a changed man and that he loved Innocence probably more than Promise did. But before he could even concentrate on getting his son's approval he had unfinished business with a dirty ass cop.

Getting inside of Detective Barns house was a piece of cake for him. Diamond had been so giddy lately she never noticed when her keys went missing the day she was invited out to lunch with Dre and Pops at Yours Truly family restaurant on Shaker Square. She went on and on about how Barns wasn't so bad and how she didn't think he had anything to do with Divine's spot. She didn't notice that Dre had excused himself from the table. It was a plus for Pops that there was a hardware shop right on the corner of 126st and Buckeye where Dre went to have copies of her keys made.

Pops stepped inside of Barns house noticing it was spotless. He knew that was courtesy of Diamond because he saw the cop transform into a junkie within a matter of months.

He quickly walked up the stairs to where he believed the bedroom to be, knowing that Barns was somewhere past out because he practically knew his doping schedule also because he knew the last batch of heroin he sent his way was potent enough to have him damn near over dosing but not dead. He wanted him to feel the bullet he was going to put between his eyes. He proceeded to ease open the door and sure enough there the dirty cop lay nodded out with a needle sticking out of his arm.

That's even better for me. Pops thought to himself. He made his way over to the bed quickly and began to tie Barns arms to the bed post.

Barns began to come out of his nod slurring, "What's going on? Who the fuck are you?"

"Who I am is not your concern. Who you are is a dirty filthy ass pig and I don't like filthy ass pigs."

Barns tried to yank his arms but it was too late they both were tied tight and now he could feel his legs stretched out and being tied to the bottom bed post. He felt now was a good time to start pleading for his life.

"Man I don't know what you're talking about but if I took something from you I will gladly give it back. Just don't kill me man."

Pops stopped what he was doing for one moment shook his head then went back to work. "You don't know what I'm talking about but if you took something from me. Pig do you hear yourself. You just admitted that you go around taking things that don't belong to you." He chuckled this time, "I'm sorry to say but your filthy pig ways has come to an end. You finally robbed the wrong motherfuckers."

There was no more time for conversation he had a job to complete. He pulled his gun out of the small of his back then walked to the top of the bed looking down at Barns. He was so excited that he had tons of adrenaline rushing threw his veins. Not doing any gruesome torture in a while had him light weight getting turned on.

He smiled down at Barns then lifted his gun and shot him dead between the eyes. Taking a towel that was laying on the night stand he wrapped it around one of his gloved hands then proceeded to sop up some of the blood that was trailing down Barns face. He wrote in big letters with the blood on the wall, DIRTY FILTHY ASS PIG.

Pops gladly walked out of the room feeling as if he left a message for the next round of dirty cops. To him it was a beautiful sight, Barns laying there with a needle sticking out of his arm, tied to the bed with a bullet between his eyes.

Now he had to make it to the basement where his little birdie told him where the stuff will be. Once he made it to the basement and to what had seemed to be a storage unit he couldn't believe his eyes. *This dirty muthafucka been robbing niggas for a long time,* he thought. Even though he could have easily took more than he came for he didn't, he knew that being greedy is what fucks a lot of people up, staying longer than they should at a crime scene. He also wanted evidence of Barns being a dirty cop left behind. So he left out of Barns house with what he was sent there for, two large black Nike duffle bags with Divine's dope and money inside. He thought her bags would be on the light side but they weren't, he guessed the Detective never made it to her stash cause he had so much more stored in his house.

TWENTY SIX

Divine hated to leave out of the house knowing that Promise wasn't doing so well but she promised her brother she would meet up with him and she also had to pick Knowledge up from his father. She figured she would kill two birds with one stone by having Jay ride with her while she went to retrieve her son. She sat outside of his newest trap spot watching him bark orders to his minions so they wouldn't fuck up in his absence. Smiling on the inside *this nigga looking like a boss.*

He hopped in his sister's car leaning over giving her a big hug. "Damn Sis, a nigga been missing you. What's been up with you?"

"Nothing much, trying to take care of my family that's it really."

"I feel that. So where we headed to?"

"I need to go pick Knowledge up then we can grab a quick bite to eat after that I need to get home."

"That's what's up! I ain't seen my nephew in a minute."

"I know that's why I came to grab you first so we can spend a little time."

"Oh Sis, I know what I've been meaning to ask you. Have you talked to Daddy? I've been trying to get at him for minute now. I know we can go awhile without talking to each other but shit it's been damn near two years now. And even though we don't get at each other all like that the nigga still answers his phone when I call, now all I get when I call is his voicemail on the first ring."

"Come on now Bro, you know me and dad ain't that close so nawl I haven't talk to him. Actually the last time I had spoken with him was on the phone when Knowledge was born. He said he was going to come see him but that never happened. Shit I ain't thought about it since. But I will see if I can get in contact with him also."

"That's what's up Sis."

She looked over at her little brother noticing he was truly concerned about their father. Some days she did think about him hating that she had him killed because she did have other siblings that were close to him. But then some days she said fuck it, it was what it was. Then she thought how in the hell was his phone still on after these past couple of years. Then again that was her father. Whoever name the phone was in must be still paying the bill hoping one day he would answer. She smiled to herself *he did fuck with some delusional ass women.*

Snapping her out of her trance she heard Jay ask her about Cherokee. She looked over at him noticing he had that same dumb smile on his face when he thought he was getting over on somebody.

"Jay why the fuck are you asking me about Cherokee?"

"Damn Sis you ain't got to curse a nigga out. I was just making conversation. I only asked because I use to see her sometimes when I went in the bank but I don't see her in there anymore, that's all."

She glanced over at him knowing he was lying through his teeth. Him asking about Cherokee out of the blue like that, yeah right it was something else to it.

"Well that's because they transferred her to another branch and I don't think it's appropriate to be inquiring about Sincere's bitch."

"Yeah I got you. That's that man's woman so I'll stay in my lane."

"Thank you."

She drove all the way to Jamal's house in silence praying that her little brother wasn't the kind of snake her brain was now making him out to be.

After dealing with Jamal's ranting and raving about how he wants to have more time with his son she finally made it back across town to drop Jay off. Seeing as though she was on Cedar she decided she would take Knowledge to visit her favorite lady.

When the two stepped out of the car at her grandmother's house Divine couldn't stop herself from laughing. Knowledge walked up the driveway to the window instead of the door to tell his grandma hi. It was so cute to watch her baby boy converse with his great-grandmother through her liquor window. She finally picked him up so they could go inside to talk. The moment she put him down he raced to give his grandma a hug.

"Hey grandma!"

She picked him up and hugged him tight, "Hey Boo-Man, what you been up to?"

All he did was snicker.

They made their way out of the bedroom to the dining room where Divine was sitting looking through the latest tabloid that was sitting on the table. Before her grandmother could sit in her favorite seat good, there was a tap on the bedroom window. She all most fell out her chair laughing when she heard Knowledge at the window saying "What can I get you" and yes her grandmother let him continue with the transaction with her assistance of course. *My son go' be something terrible when he grow up* was all she could say.

After talking to her favorite for a while Divine decided to take a quick nap on the couch, leaving her son to enjoy his time with his grandmother.

She was sleeping soundly when she felt Knowledge nudging her arm. Rolling over she couldn't help but smile at his handsome big face.

"What's good little man?"

He lifted her phone to her face, "Your phone mommy."

"Thanks Boo-Man"

She looked at her phone noticing she had six missed calls, five from Promise and one from Pops. Then she saw the icon letting her know she had a text. *Damn I must have been tired as hell to not have heard none of this.* She read her text messages first.

Don: I don't feel to good Doll

She immediately called him back.

"Yeah" He answered a tad aggravated because she hadn't been answering her phone.

"Baby I am so sorry, I brought Knowledge to see my grandmother and I fell asleep on the couch but I'm on my way right now."

"You sure that's why you wasn't answering your phone?"

"I'm positive Don. I didn't even realize I was that tired. I still didn't even hear my phone. I guess Knowledge got tired of hearing it so he woke me up and gave it to me."

He felt a little bad because he knew why she was so tired. He had been tossing and turning so much at night keeping both of them awake.

"Yeah I can understand that. Get you some more rest while you're there then go holla at Pops before you come home, he says he has something for you."

"Okay, but how do you feel now?"

"I'm good but I'll be better once you and my babies are home so try not to take too long."

"K, see you in a minute."

TWENTY SEVEN

Promise had become so restless at night. He tossed and turned all night long ever since he felt that dope in his system. When he lay in the bed all he could think about was the wonderful feeling he got when the heroin invaded his blood stream. He tried and tried to be strong but his body wasn't allowing him to be. He kept telling himself he only needed to feel that feeling one more time then maybe he could get some rest, just one more time. He eased out of bed heading to the walk-in closet. He dressed quickly throwing on an around the house jogging suit then made his way over to the bed to give Divine a kiss on the forehead whispering, "I'm sorry in her ear."

She tried to grab his hand but he walked away.

"Don't do it Don," was the last thing he heard his Queen say before he walked out of their bedroom at four o'clock in the morning.

Before he could sit down in his truck good he heard his cell phone ringing. He tried to ignore it knowing it was Divine but she was being very persistent.

"Doll I tried, but I promise you it's only going to be one time." He answered as he put his truck in reverse.

"I know Baby, but let me go get it for you. I don't want you to get caught out there slipping somewhere all in another zone. Or I don't want to take any chances of you getting pulled over so come back in the house." She breathed heavily in the phone, "Bottom line is I don't want you doing that shit in the streets, that's something to be done at home behind closed doors."

He hung up his phone and shifted the gear in park leaving the truck running. He walked into the house through the side door as she walked out the front.

Divine drove down Chagrin with her heart and her mind all over the place. She shed a thousand tears as she drove because she couldn't believe what she was going to do. All she knew is her King was sick and if she wasn't going to get it he sure in the hell was. The last thing she needed was for her King's business to be out in the streets.

She didn't want to go to the trap spot to get what he needed because then she would take the risk of someone seeing her and wondering why she was there that time of the morning. Therefore she had to take a trip to one of her honey comb hide outs all the way on the other side of town. Once she reached her destination and got what she needed she realized he was going to need tools. Now where in the fuck was she going to get that shit from without someone being suspect? Picking up her phone she shot him a text.

Me: What about tools?

Don: Not needed you know I really don't like needles anyway.

Making her way back home with the clock striking 5:10 she was happy to see him passed out on the couch sleeping like a baby. He was stretched out snoring and everything.

Instead of waking him up to do the unthinkable she grabbed herself a cover and got comfortable on the love seat falling fast asleep.

"Wake your mommy up Treasure, tell her breakfast is ready." She heard Promise tell their daughter while she was asleep. Before Treasure could tap her shoulder she picked her up and threw her on the love seat with her then began smothering her with kisses.

Treasure tried to fight her off, "Mommy stop."

Her words may have been saying mommy stop but her laughing encouraged Divine to keep going.

Finally letting her daughter up for some air she made her way to the bathroom to brush her teeth then to her bedroom to get out of the track suit she had threw on. After changing into some house clothes she noticed the dime baggy that she had brought back a couple of hours ago. It was sitting on top of Promise's dresser empty. He must have gone inside of her purse when she was sleeping.

Making her way back to the kitchen she sat down at the table studying his every move. He didn't seem like he was moving in slow motion or as if he was in another zone. He actually seemed to be acting like his normal self. *Maybe he flushed it* she thought then proceeded to eat her breakfast.

Cherokee was awakened out of a deep sleep with Sincere kissing on her stomach. She looked down at him then stroked his handsome face lightly with her fingers.

"Babe what are you doing?"

"I'm kissing my baby."

She smiled at him, "Well let me go brush my teeth because I would rather have some kisses on my lips verses my stomach."

"I'm not talking about you. I'm talking about my baby inside of you." He responded looking up at her.

By force of nature she automatically touched her stomach.

"Babe what are you talking about. I'm not pregnant."

"Rephrase that Kee, you mean you don't know if you're pregnant because you haven't taken a test yet. But don't think I haven't noticed that your period is three days late and all you have been doing lately is sleeping."

"Well I did notice that also but I was going to give my period a couple of more days before I told you. I didn't want us thinking too far ahead you know. I mean look at you now rubbing and kissing my stomach talking about your baby." She grabbed his hand so he could stop rubbing. "I just want to be one hundred percent sure before we get our hopes up."

He hopped in the bed next to her getting comfortable. "Well if that's the case gone in the bathroom and start pissing then. I got three different brands all sitting on the sink waiting on you lil mama."

She looked over at him and smiled saying "Only you Babe, only you."

She couldn't help but smile when she went in the bathroom and saw he had taken them all out of their packages and had them lined up. *I guess that means he wants me to pee on all of them.* After soaking up each test and sitting them on the back of the toilet she figured she'll take care of her morning hygiene while she waited for the results. She brushed her teeth, washed her face, her pussy, and her ass. After she dried her private areas she peeked at the test with all three screaming at her the same answer. She walked out of the bathroom with a sad look on her face making the smile Sincere had on his turn upside down.

Sliding in bed next to him she asked "why the sad face daddy?"

"I don't know, I guess I was hoping you were pregnant."

Smiling brightly this time and placing his hand on her stomach she asked again, "Like I asked before, why the sad face daddy?"

"Stop playing wit' me Kee. Are we pregnant or what?"

This time she lay on top of him and began placing soft kisses on his lips. "Earlier I told you I wanted you to kiss my lips and now since I've got that you can go back to kissing your baby."

Words couldn't express how happy Sincere was at that moment. He never really put any thought into becoming a father any time soon but from the first day she missed her period it was the only thing he thought about.

He picked her up sliding her body up his so that he was face to face with her stomach kissing every inch of it. After giving his baby some attention he slid Cherokee all the way up so her pussy was now in his face. He tapped her on her ass cheek, "Playtime over for real Kee, what we got now is death 'til we part. Do you understand me?"

She looked down at him, "Yes Sincere."

With that he eased her down on his face so he could give sweet kisses to her pussy.

TWENTY EIGHT

After being in the house for the past couple of weeks Promise felt it was time for him to get some fresh air. His first stop was to the car wash so he could get his Suburban shining right. While his truck was getting washed he thought about texting his heart to see what she and the kids were up to then he thought against it. He wasn't a big fan of the texting thing and he did miss hearing her voice on the phone.

When Divine heard Promise ring tone coming through her phone she wondered why he was calling so soon, he had just left the house.

"Hey you," she answered praying that everything was okay.

"What you doing?"

"Nothing much, me and the kids are watching Happy Feet for the one hundredth time."

He gave a slight chuckle. "That's what's up!"

"Is everything cool?" She asked him with much concern in her voice.

"Everything cool Mommy, I'm just missing the hell out of you."

By him saying that put a huge smile on her face. If nothing else in this world she loved her man to death.

"Why you cheesing so big? I can hear your smile through the phone."

"Whatever, you think you know me so well. I'm just happy you're missing me so soon. It seems like you've been a little distant these past couple of days. You've been staying in the room by yourself a lot lately."

"I know Doll, I apologize. A lot of shit has been on my mind and I'm trying to get a handle on this bullshit. You feel me?"

She inhaled deeply because she didn't know how he was going to react to her next statement.

"Nawl I don't feel you, seeing as though you been light weight indulging in the bullshit. I've been seeing the baggies you call yourself hiding in your top drawer."

"I only put them there because I don't want to put them in the trash and the kids get a hold of them. When I know I'm going to take the trash out is when I clear the drawer. Doll, you do the laundry so you should know by now I'm not trying to hide anything from you. And you just said that like it's been on your mind for a while, so why haven't you said shit if it was bothering you? You know what don't even answer that. I'm about to call Innocence so she can come up there and sit with the kids then I want you to come to me. That's cool wit' you?"

"Yeah, that's cool," she sniffled.

"And stop that crying. I don't want my babies to see you like that, okay."

She hung up the phone wiping the tears out of her eyes then looked at the kids as they watched their movie not paying her any attention. She looked up at the ceiling, *Lord please protect my family. Promise most of all.*

Instead of calling his mother he figured he'd shoot over there since he was right up the street and his truck had just gotten finished. The moment he walked threw his mother's door he was met with the biggest surprised. Diamond jumped up in his face screaming and beating him in his chest.

"Promise I know it was you. It was nobody but you, why the fuck would you do him like that?"

He grabbed her hands and pushed her down on the couch. That didn't keep her down though she jumped back up in one point two seconds and started screaming and hitting on him again.

This time he raised his hand at her, "Diamond I swear to God if you hit me one more time I'm going to smack the shit out of you."

She knew her big brother had no problems with putting her in her place so she stopped assaulting him.

"Now what the fuck are you talking about?" He questioned her mad as shit.

"You know good and damn well what I'm talking about. Why you have to do him like that Brother?"

He knew by her calling him brother she was really hurt. She hasn't called him that since she was about nine years old.

Walking up to her he embraced her with a hug. "Diamond you know I love you." He tilted her chin so she could look up at him. "But I have no idea what you are talking about."

He knew not to admit anything to his sister because she was to emotionally attach to Barns. For all he knew she could be standing there wired up trying to trap him.

From his peripheral he noticed his mother getting her things together like she was about to leave.

"Ma, where you going?"

"Divine called and told me that you wanted me to watch the kids so I'm on my way up there."

"Okay, thanks ma."

"Anytime baby."

He turned his attention back to Diamond.

"Sis I love you but you got to hold yourself together, okay."

She sniffled some more replying, "Okay"

After getting Diamond squared away he texted Divine to let her know to meet him at his favorite spot.

Getting settled in his truck his cell phone began to ring. He looked at his screen noticing it was his mother.

"Yeah Ma"

"I talked to Pops and he told me everything so your sister is not to be trusted."

"I know."

"Okay baby as long as you know. And why I have you on the phone do you think it would be a problem if I take him with me so he can spend some time with them also?"

He closed his eyes shaking his head. He hated the thought of Pops being around his mother. Pops being around him was cool, being around Divine was cool, him even being around his grandbabies was cool, but he did not want him around his mother. Then he thought of what Divine told him, it wasn't his decision to make.

"Ma you know what, you're a grown woman so if that's what you want it's fine with me."

Innocence smiled because she knew it was hard for her child to accept that the man that she loved was the same man that raped her.

"Thanks son, I promise you everything is going to be okay with us."

"I ain't worried about that Ma. If some shady shit go down you already know what it is."

"I know son and thank you once again."

Divine pulled up to the valet service at the Inter-Continental Hotel. After giving the valet attendant her car keys she made her way to the front desk.

"Promise Green room please."

The nice lady typed on her computer keyboard then turned to retrieve the key card to the Presidential Suite.

"Thank you very much." Divine politely said to the woman then made her way to her King.

Entering the room she was a little surprised to see it wasn't decked out fit for a Queen as usual.

"What, I don't get the royal treatment this trip?" She stated as she embraced him with a hug

He kissed the top of her forehead. "I didn't have time to set up. I just really wanted you here so we can relax and have a change of atmosphere."

"I can understand that Daddy."

He led her to the bathroom where he had a hot bubble bath waiting for her in the Jacuzzi style tub. Undressing her slowly he made sure he touched every inch of her body. He helped her inside the tub then settled himself behind her. Picking up the wash cloth he began to sprinkle water down the front of her.

"I miss you Doll"

"I miss you too Baby. So tell me, what are we going to do about that dumb shit you been doing?" She asked as the first tear escaped her eye.

He cupped her chin so he could turn her head to face him. It broke his heart to see the tears coming down her face. If it was one thing he hated was to see Divine cry. She was such a strong person so to see her cry meant she was hurting badly. The last thing he wanted was to be the monster that was the cause of her pain.

"Baby I don't need that shit. You know you're my only drug of choice."

Staring at him in his beautiful brown eyes she wanted so desperately to believe him but she knew she couldn't. She was no match for the heroin that has now taken control over his mind and body. No matter how hard he tries to it was going to be an everyday struggle for the both of them until he decides he wants to seek professional help. But the sincerity he was now showing her at that moment was enough for her to believe his lie, even if was only for one moment.

"I can't tell I'm your drug of choice. You haven't touched your heaven in exactly seven days. Shame on you Don, what you trying to tell me you're not the keeper of these gates anymore?"

He moved his hand down to play with her middle. "Don't play with me Divine Nanette. I don't give a fuck what I'm going through, this pussy belongs to me. Do you understand me?"

Instead of bowing down like she always does she took control.

"No I don't understand. I guess you have to prove to me that this pussy is yours and I mean all yours. Daddy doesn't want his kitty cat straying away from home now do he?"

"You know what Doll, you playing with fire so I seriously advise you to stop." He responded to her last statement as he applied pressure to her chin.

This time she pushed his hand away from her face then turned to straddle him. Placing her hand on his manhood she began to stroke it until it stood at attention. She eased herself down on his dick then grabbed his chin pulling his face to hers.

"I'm not the one playing with fire, you are. And if you don't get that shit together real soon you won't be feeling your heaven anytime soon."

As she began riding him she applied a little pressure to his chin then pressed her lips against his ear.

"I'm going to say this one time and one time only,

I am your Queen and I refuse to allow you to pump in and out of me with a doped up dick. Now the question is do you understand me?"

He didn't know when the tables turned but now he knew why she came every time he was aggressive with her. In three minutes flat he was grabbing her around the waist cumming inside of her promising her that he understood.

TWENTY NINE

An entire two months had passed and it seemed as if all the drama had died down so Divine thought it would be a good idea to invite the Fam out for drinks, on her of course. They haven't been together as a whole in like forever because everybody was off doing their own side things. She was taking trips to EC more than ever now seeing as though she had to take her son out there on some days and on others she was transporting cocaine to his father. Then when she wasn't doing that she was on Cedar supervising Jay. Sincere was handling business on Superior with his new dude Quan and venturing down in the projects pumping them niggas up with x-pills. Promise was doing she didn't know what and she was starting to not even give a fuck. Dre was handling Kinsman and doing a damn good job at it. She knew it was just a matter of time before he took over Promise's reign, with her and Sincere at his side of course.

After dropping her kids off to their grandparents she made her way back home so she could get ready for the night. Of course when she had gotten back home Promise was doing what he does best, sit on the side of the bed zoned out pretending to be watching TV.

She stood on the side of him looking down at the side of his face. "I'm about to go get in the shower."

Never looking up at her he replied, "I'll be in there in a minute."

She walked into the bathroom never responding to his last statement because she knew it was a lie. He hasn't washed his heaven in damn near two months so she knew he wasn't going to start then, not while his new bitch had a hold of him.

Instead of taking a shower she decided to take a bath so she could relax and clear her mind. She honestly didn't know what she was going to do about Promise. He hasn't touched her nor has he spent any time with the kids. She thinks the only time he left the house was when he going to dig in one of his stash spots. She wasn't a fool so she been separated her drugs from his. She figured if he wanted to toot his nose he was going to do it with his own shit. She was not allowing him to dip off into hers too.

Once she was squeaky clean she made her way back to the bedroom and that nigga was still sitting there in the same spot. Not allowing him to interfere with her night she ignored him by going in their walk-in closet. She figured she would dress inside of there because she was so tired of screaming at his ass. If he didn't care about what he was doing to his own self then why in the hell should she.

When she stepped out the closet she could tell she caught his attention for two point two seconds. Well she could say she didn't catch his attention but her outfit sure in the hell did.

Her body was laced in a black fitted jumpsuit with a strapped back. She wasn't leaving anything to the imagination that night. She only put the jumpsuit on thinking that would get him off his ass and get dress so he could be there standing guard all night making sure no one touched her, but that didn't happen. Saying fuck it she went back in the closet to put her accessories on. She was not allowing him to destroy her night because he chose to be a dope head.

Leaving out of the house she realized she had a text message from Sincere.

Twin: Me and Kee only stopping through for a quick sec because we had already made other plans. And I have some good news to tell you.

Me: Cool

When she walked through the Sa'rah House doors the first person she saw was Jamal. *Now what the hell he doing on this side of town,* she asked herself. Not wanting to seem like she was acting funny she walked over to him embracing him with a hug.

"What's good BM?"

"Nothing much, so what are you doing over this way?"

"My cousin having a party in here tonight, you know he a Harvard nigga for real." He replied as he pointed in the direction of his peoples.

"That's cool. Well let me get over to my folks."

Grabbing her by her waist he stopped her in mid stride. "What you can't have a drink wit' yo baby daddy first?"

"Of course I can, just give me a minute to go kick it with my people first."

When she made over it to where the Fam had situated themselves for the night Dre was the first one at her neck.

"Doll who the fuck is that nigga grabbing all on you?"

"He's an old friend, ain't shit serious."

He looked over in Jamal's direction with his face turned up. "Old friend my ass, this nigga staring over here like he got some ties wit' you or something."

She put a reassuring hand on his shoulder, "Dre for real calm down, we just go way back that's all."

This time he turned his screwed up face in her direction staring her in the face. "Where the fuck Promise at? And do he know you out here dressed like this?"

Dre was really starting to aggravate her. Her purpose of getting out of the house was to have a couple of drinks and to relax, not get harassed by baby Promise standing in her face.

"He at home, maybe he's coming maybe he's not but right now I don't give a fuck. So please calm down lil bro I'm trying to enjoy myself tonight." With that she hugged him then walked over to the bar to order her first shot of Remy VSOP.

After throwing back her second shot she saw her flesh and blood brother walking her way. Feeling a little tipsy from the liquor she grabbed him throwing her arms around him giving him a big hug.

"What's good Jay? I'm glad you made it up here."

"Now you already know I wasn't go' miss a chance to kick it with my big sis."

"That's what I'm talking about. Come on come sit at the bar with me."

She ordered herself another shot and a glass of water and ordered Jay some Ciroc and orange juice. After politicking with her little brother for a while she made her way over to Jamal to have a drink with him like she promised.

Jamal couldn't help but have that big Chester the cat smile on his face when he noticed Divine walking over to him. Even though he was still feeling a certain kind of way about the whole ordeal with his son, she was still his nigga. If he didn't miss anything else he missed her coming over to the house chilling on the porch with him and making her laugh all day. Yeah he saw her when she came to drop lil man off and he saw her when they were conducting business but it was nothing like spending some one on one kickin' it time with her. She had to be one of the most down to earth people that he knew. Once she made it over to him he wasted no time telling her what he was feeling.

"Vines I know I see you a good two times a week but a nigga misses you for real."

She smiled at him because she truly understood how he felt. Not only did she miss chopping it up with her nigga she missed getting some attention from a man period. And why not let Jamal be the one to feel that void, she did already have a baby by him.

"Yeah I can say I miss you too. Maybe when I bring Knowledge over there this Sunday we can go grab a bite to eat or something while he chill with your grandmother."

Grabbing her and pulling her close to him he whispered in her ear, "Yeah we can do that and after maybe we can shoot to my spot so I can eat me some dessert, got me over here drooling at the mouth. I ain't say you can show off my goods like this."

She kissed the side of his face, "If that's your way of saying I look nice then thank you. And the eating dessert thing sure does sounds like a plan to me."

As soon as she turned to walk away from him she noticed Sincere and Cherokee coming through the door. She didn't even let them make it half way to the bar before she bombarded both of them with hugs.

"I'm so glad y'all came. I was starting to think y'all weren't coming." She explained to them.

"Now you know I was coming to see about my twin, not to mention I told you I had some good news to tell you."

"Oh yeah I forgot about that. So what's the good news?" She asked as she shifted from side to side in anticipation.

Sincere put his hands on the small of both of their backs ushering them towards the bar. "Calm yourself down, I'll tell you over a drink."

When they approached the bar and Jay turned to greet them with that charming smile of his Cherokee stopped in her tracks trying to catch her breath.

Sincere looked down at her with concern written all over his face. "Kee Baby, you okay?"

"I'm okay Babe, just lost my balance a little. But can we please not stay to long like you said?"

He bent to kiss her on her juicy lips, "Anything you say Kee."

Getting Cherokee settled on a bar stool Sincere ordered their drinks without even acknowledging Jay's presence. Divine noticed the growing male testosterone between her two brothers but she wasn't going to dwell on it at the moment. She was going to very soon though because the way they acted around each other was ridiculous. Especially with Sincere because he knew the truth so why he was treating his younger brother like he wasn't shit was beyond her.

Once the bartender arrived with their drinks Divine noticed Cherokee didn't have liquor but a tall glass of orange juice. And if it was one thing she knew about Cherokee was that the girl could drink, she especially loved wine.

Pointing to the glass of OJ she asked, "Does this mean what I think it means?"

Cherokee smiled at her saying, "Yes it does."

Divine started to jump up down, "Oh my God, Kee I am so happy for you." She then began to hug her. "I'm going to be an auntie."

Sincere cleared his throat, "Damn Twin I don't get none, I do believe I put all the work in."

She turned and started hugging him. "I'm sorry. You can get some love too."

Getting her composure together she stood between the two. "So when is the due date?"

"August third and I'm hoping it's a boy, two females around the house is enough." Sincere responded as he kissed Cherokee on the cheek.

After the three celebrated Divine felt it was a good time to introduce Sincere to Jamal seeing as though they were all now running in the same circle with that white girl.

The moment she introduced Sincere to Jamal he knew automatically that was the nigga Promise had told him about. The resemblance was crazy. His nephew looked just like the nigga. Either way that was his sisters business and she and Promise was already dealing with it so who was he to say shit. He was now more concern with the way Jay kept smiling in Cherokee's direction and how she looked uncomfortable trying to ignore him. Focusing more on her he noticed she looked as if she were hyperventilating trying to catch her breath. Then he looked back over at Jay looking as if he was enjoying the torture she seemed to be under.

It didn't take Divine long at all to notice that something or someone had Sincere's attention which made her look in the same direction. And it didn't take long for her to realize what was going through his head because it was now going through hers.

She watched in slow motion as he started walking towards Jay. Then when she saw him easing his gun off his hip she sprung into action. She ran past him throwing herself in front of Jay.

"Not here Sin, please not here. It's too many eyes Twin." She pleaded with him knowing that the only thing that was on his mind was getting his hands on Jay. Then Jay wasn't making it better giving Sincere the 'yeah I fucked yo bitch face'.

"Move the fuck out the way Doll!"

She spoke through clenched teeth, "Not here Sin." Then she gestured with her head for him to look around.

Her doing that made him take note to all the spectators standing around. It seemed that the entire bar had stopped moving. He looked over at the door noticing people leaving then he looked over at Dre and their goons seeing that they all had their pistols posted at their sides. He then looked at Cherokee crying her eyes out conforming what he was already thinking.

"We got to get out of here Sin. You know the police are probably on their way. Let's go Twin you can handle this another day." He heard Divine say.

He walked up to Cherokee and whispered in her ear, "Bitch I'm going to kill you."

He then pointed his gun in Jay's direction, "You already know lil nigga."

With that he was out the door with the Kinsman County Family in tow.

Divine turned to look at Jay. "Nigga take that dumb ass smile off yo face. Do you realize what the fuck you have done?" She griped at him.

She then turned to Cherokee who was sitting there looking like she had already lost her life five minutes ago. "That goes for you too."

She picked up her clutch off the bar and headed towards the door. Once she made it to her car she turned to see Cherokee was on her heels.

"I swear to God if my brother's baby wasn't inside of you I'll leave your ass here. Get in the damn car."

By the time they made it to the red light at Lee and Harvard Cherokee started pleading her case.

"Doll I swear to God I didn't ever want anybody to find out."

Divine just looked over at her with a disgusted look on her face.

"Sincere is going to kill me. Oh my God, what have I done?" She cried out loud more so to herself.

Her crying was starting to get on Divine's last nerve. "Cherokee calm down. He's not going to touch you as long as you're carrying his baby. So please calm the fuck down so I can think."

Sniffling she shook her head okay. Then she thought about what Divine had said earlier. "Divine this is Sincere's baby."

"I know that."

"Well I was only telling you because when we were outside the bar you said I was pregnant by your brother."

This time when she stopped at the light on Lee and Chagrin she looked over at Cherokee, "That's because Sincere is my brother and he's also Jay's."

Hearing that made Cherokee eyes get wide as saucers.

Busting a right on Chagrin when the light turned green Divine chuckled. "Yeah you fucked brothers and now you done started a damn war between them. So now I hope you feel like shit."

Cherokee reclined her head back on the seat crying even more thinking shit was far from what she was feeling like.

THIRTY

Driving in the direction of his home Sincere tried to wrap his brain around what had occurred. He kept telling his self it wasn't any way possible that Cherokee slept with Jay. Not his Kee Baby. She wouldn't dare betray him like that. Speeding he banged his fist repeatedly on the steering wheel. All he kept envisioning were her legs wrapped around Jay's neck. A couple times he thought he was going to throw up from the tricks his brain was playing on him.

"I'm going to kill that nigga." He screamed out loud to himself as he drove.

He wasn't in the house five minutes before he was back in his car speeding across Richmond Rd. He made it to Divine's house in record time.

Jumping out of his car he proceeded to bang on the door. "Doll, open this muthafucka up."

Speaking through the door, "Only if you promise you're not going to put your hands on her."

"Man, open up this damn door. What the fuck I look like putting my hands on her pregnant ass." This time he kicked the door. "Open this fuckin' door Doll."

Knowing he wasn't going to put his hands on Cherokee was enough for her to open the door. That and the fact she was afraid he might wake her neighbors then have the police at her damn door. And who the fuck felt like that shit.

When he got through the door he pushed past Divine and made his way over to Cherokee. He stood over her looking down at her like a mad man. Grabbing her up by the arm he pushed her towards the door then turned back around to bark at to his sister.

"Your brother is a dead man and it ain't shit you can say to save him. I'm not gone go looking for him but I'm letting you know once I see him I'm killing him on sight."

Divine stared at her big brother because she knew it was nothing she could do or say to save Jay. He had committed the ultimate betrayal. Not only did he fuck Sincere's woman, he raped her. It didn't matter that it started out consensual what mattered most was when she came to her senses she said no. There was no way around that.

"It's fucked up cause I can't even begin to defend him, but what I can say is that whenever you do run into him please remember that he's your brother too and she put herself in that fucked up predicament."

"Fuck nawl, I ain't go' remember shit. And it don't matter what she put herself in that nigga knew what the fuck he was up to in the beginning. He knew exactly what he was doing now his young ass go' pay." He replied as he walked out of her door slamming it behind him.

Divine knew she was wrong for saying Cherokee did that to herself because no woman deserved to be raped. By Cherokee explaining what happen to her months ago but not letting her know who the guy was she did feel sorry for her. But right at that moment all she wanted was for her to feel like shit even if was only for a little while. And Jay, she couldn't wait until she got her hands on him. Rape, seriously. And Sincere's girl at that, he had to know he was dead wrong. She knew Jay didn't care for Sincere but she didn't think it was that bad. If she had she would have been let him know that Sincere was his brother a long time ago. Maybe if he knew he wouldn't have done what he did. Then she thought against it. He was a snake just like their father he would have done the bullshit anyway.

Saying fuck it to herself she made her way to her bedroom so she could get some sleep. The Remy plus the drama had her head swimming in all kinds of directions. When she walked through her bedroom door and saw Promise laid out sleeping soundly she instantly got sick. How the hell could he have been sleeping through that commotion? His ass was doped up of course. She knew then it was time for him to seek professional help and if he didn't want it then it was time for him to get the fuck out of her house and far away from her and her kids. *Anything could have been happening to me and this nigga wouldn't have heard shit with his junkie ass,* she thought to herself as she made her way to sleep in the guest room.

All the way home the only thing that could be heard was Cherokee crying.

"Kee I swear to God on my life, if you don't stop that fuckin' crying I will put my hands on you."

Hearing him say that silenced her cries fast. But it did nothing for the tears that were still trailing down her face. By the time they made it home her face was so swollen from crying Sincere didn't even want to yell at her anymore. He hated to see her hurting.

"Go in the bathroom and clean yourself up Kee."

He shook his head because he could hear her sniffling all the way to the bathroom. Making his way to the kitchen to make himself a drink he figured he should give his sister a call.

Seeing Sincere's number come through her phone sobered Divine up just enough so she could hear what he had to say.

"I guess I should say thank you for getting her out of the bar safe. I know you only did it because of my seed inside of her. I guess I should also say I'm sorry for screaming at you and disturbing your household. But I still mean what the fuck I said about that nigga Sis."

Hearing the sadness in his voice and knowing how he had to be broken up inside did something to her heart.

"Where Kee at?"

"In the bathroom cleaning up her face, that damn girl cried all the way home."

"Yeah, she cried all the way to my house too. And for the record I didn't get her out of the bar. When I made it to my car she was already behind me on my heels. Twin you know that girl loves you right?"

"Yeah I know but once my baby is born she better hope and pray I don't bury her ass."

"Sin listen I know this isn't my place to tell you because for one I promised Kee I wouldn't and for two I don't think she will stop crying long enough to explain her case to you."

Her saying that caught his attention fast, "Speak Doll."

She went on to explain to him everything Cherokee had told her about what had happened between her and Jay. How at first he was just a listening ear because Sincere was out doing his thing paying her no attention. How she tried to reach out to Divine but she way to busy doing her thing so she didn't have time for her either. She explained how at first it was only lunches, dinners, and conversations. She also told him how at first she did get weak and allow him to do some things to her then she changed her mind and then that's when things got ugly.

He interrupted her, "Wait Doll, you mean to tell me you knew it was Jay all along?"

"No Sincere when she told me the story she omitted the name telling me she didn't want to cause any trouble. But I swear to you not one time would I have ever thought it was Jay. I promise you that. I'm going to put it to you like this Sin, out of two years she messed up one time. And no matter what you have to remember she was raped. He's our brother but that nigga was foul for what he did. Rather he knew of y'all relationship or not, him raping that girl was dead wrong because at the end of the day he knew she was your woman. I can't tell you what the issue is with y'all two but I can tell you he don't give a fuck about you like you don't give a fuck about him." She paused for a moment. "Sin, don't let that shady ass nigga tear up your happy home. Man your face was lit up like a Christmas tree when I figured out your good news. Don't let that nigga steal your joy from you Brother, for real."

"Yeah I hear you Twin."

"But do you understand me?"

"I got you. I know what I'm dealing with over here. I know this girl love my dirty drawls and I know what part I played to make her turn to that faggot ass nigga anyway. We go' be okay. Hay since we're on some serious shit, what's up with Promise?"

She turned over in the bed letting the tears escape from her eyes. "Do you really want to know?"

"I asked didn't I? Wait before you start though Sis, let me go check on this girl."

"Okay"

She didn't know where the Sis thing was coming from with Sincere but she liked it better than Twin. She guessed it was time for them to stop pretending and face facts, they were brother and sister. And it was time the world knew it to so they wouldn't have any more problems.

Sincere walked inside his bedroom only to find Cherokee fully dressed lying on top of the covers still crying. He walked over and sat down beside her.

"Kee why are you laying here still dressed and why the hell are you still crying?"

She shrugged her shoulders, "I don't know what else to do. I'm scared Sincere."

Even though he was so angry with her he didn't like seeing her so emotional. He caressed the side of her face.

"What are you scared of Kee?"

She sniffled some more, "Of what you're going to do to me."

He chuckled at that thought, "You mean to tell me you haven't realized by now that I'm not going to put my hands on you. Divine already explained everything to me and she let you keep your pass in my life so if I were you I'd be thanking her sometime soon."

"So y'all are real sisters and brothers, huh?"

"Yes we are but that ain't for everybody to know. You got that?"

"Yes Sincere."

"Now get up, go get in the shower and be ready for me when I get back in this bed okay."

She gave him a slight smile shaking her head yes.

"By the way I'm not going to hurt you now, but after you have my baby I'm going to whoop that ass. You ain't getting away with this shit that easy."

When he said that she started crying all over again, "Come on now Kee, I don't know how much of this crying I can take. You know what you did so you're going to accept the consequences that come along with that shit."

"But Baby I'm sorry and I promise won't let anything like that ever happen again."

"Trust me I know it won't because if it does you're going to be one dead female. Now gone and get in the shower so you can get some rest, stressing my baby out and shit with all that damn crying."

By the time he made it back downstairs to his phone he noticed Divine had hung up.

Calling her back he asked, "What the hell you hang up for, I said hold on didn't I."

"Boy you was gone for so long I didn't know if y'all was having a makeup session or not. And I definitely wasn't staying on the phone for that, anyway how she doing?"

Getting comfortable on the sofa he grabbed the remote and turned the TV on. "Her cry baby ass cool, I swear Sis I ain't never seen a female cry that damn much."

She laughed at his statement as she sat up in bed. "That's ya mans," she said imitating DMX from the movie Belly.

He cracked up laughing because she was horrible at imitating DMX but she always tried. "Right, anyway getting back to my nigga."

She went on to tell him the chain of events since the day he came home from the hospital leaving nothing out. She even told him how she went and got the first bag for him.

"Man Sis, say you swear."

"I swear Brother, this shit I'm going through over here is crazy."

"So where that nigga at right now?"

Giving a slight chuckle she responded, "His ass in there doped the fuck up. Keep trying to act like everything cool saying he got it under control. That nigga ain't got shit under control. We ain't fucked in I don't know how long, he ain't spent no quality time with these fuckin' kids. All the nigga do is sit in that damn room tooting his fuckin' nose. Talking 'bout he don't like needles, he might as well stick that shit in his veins so his ass can gone and over dose this time. I bet you I won't try to save his ass then."

"Man slow down and catch yo breath. And you know good and well that's not how you really feel. So what we go' do about this shit? Do Innocence and Pops know?"

"Nawl they don't know. But first thing in the morning I'm going to give him an ultimatum, either he's going to let me check him into rehab or he go' get the fuck out. I ain't about to go through no junkie shit with his ass and I damn sure ain't about to put my babies through it. I don't care how much I love him."

"Damn, this shit is all fucked up. If he doesn't want the help what are you going to do about Treasure?"

She looked at the phone sideways, "That's my daughter. What you mean what I'm go' do?"

"I'm just asking. Well if you want me to come over there in the morning while y'all talk I will."

"Yeah that would be cool. I know I'm talking all this shit but I'm going to need the support. Sin I don't think anyone could ever comprehend how much I love this nigga. And my nigga, my nigga, a fuckin' junkie, now ain't that some shit."

"I know Sis, we go' handle that shit though."

By the time they got off of the phone Divine was crying her eyes out with Sincere joking with her telling her he guessed Cherokee wasn't the only cry baby in the family.

EPILOGUE

Sincere sat across from Jay's newest trap spot on 126th and Miles watching him talk some hoe brains off. He looked as his little brother boasted about nothing. To him he was a straight corn ball. He knew he promised his sister he wouldn't go looking for him but he couldn't help himself.

He hated that every time he looked at his beautiful daughter's face he saw Jay's. She looked so much like the nigga that he made Cherokee give him a paternity test. Of course she cried the whole time they were getting swabbed swearing that his daughter belonged to him. And sure enough the test came back saying that his beautiful Hope Mitchell-Green was his but he just couldn't shake the fact that she looked so much like that nigga. Truthfully she looked just like Divine, but his sister wasn't anything but a female version of Jay which meant his baby girl was also. And he didn't like that shit one bit. He knew it was no one's fault but genetics, but he still didn't like it. Family or not his faggot ass brother had to go. He pointed his finger in his direction as if he was shooting him. *Nigga you go' be dead before New Year's Eve.* He then pulled off so he could go put his plan in motion.

Divine fussed at Cherokee promising her she would never wait until the last minute to do her Christmas shopping again. She wanted to do all of her shopping online but Cherokee had to be out amongst other people. Who in the hell enjoyed being in crowded ass stores bumping into people was crazy to her. But there she was anyway out at Aurora Premium Outlets shopping her heart away.

Entering the NAUTICA store Divine vowed she wasn't going to buy Knowledge another jacket but once she got to the children's section she picked up every coat they had in his size.

Cherokee shook her head, "I thought you said he had enough coats?"

Holding one up she responded, "I know but ain't this one to cute. He go' be so handsome with this orange against his skin. Kee I think I want to take the kids to Dave and Busters for his fourth birthday. What you think?"

"That's fine with me. You know Shereé loves going out there. The little heifer be trying to throw temper tantrums when it's time for us to go. I don't think I'm going to bring Hope though."

"Girl you crazy if you think my niece not going to be there celebrating with her cousin for his birthday."

"Doll, she is only four and half months old what is she possibly going to do there?"

"Get carried by her auntie all day, that's what."

"I swear between you and Sincere she is going to be spoiled."

Walking past pushing her Divine responded, "She's a baby, she's supposed to be spoiled."

"What the hell ever. Got her thinking somebody supposed to hold her all night."

"What you complaining for, you ain't the one holding her. Her daddy is."

Poking her lip out Cherokee replied, "That's the problem her little butt cock blocking already."

Divine busted out laughing. "Don't start Kee."

"Soooo, what's up with you and Jamal?" Cherokee asked as she looked over the cutest dress for Hope.

Her hearing his name made Divine get a little bubbly eyed. "All I'm going to say is, (I love my baby daddy I'll never let him go)."

Cherokee really burst out laughing, "Doll I swear you do the worst DMX."

"Whatever Kee, so when we go' do the Miami trip? Seeing as though we had to postpone because you just had to go and get pregnant."

"That I did! And stop complaining because you know you love her more than I do. But let's try for Spring Break. You know all the niggas go' be out then."

Looking at her sideways, "Don't start any shit Kee. But Spring Break will be perfect."

"You know I'm just playing Doll. Messing around with your brother he's going to be trying to come with us."

Throwing her hand at Cherokee she said, "Girl ain't nobody thinking about him." Then she headed to the checkout line. Standing in line her phone indicated that she had a text message. After placing her items on the counter she pulled out her phone and began to read the text.

Cherokee noticed the sad look that was now on her friends face. "You okay Doll?"

Placing the phone back in her pocket she gave her a slight smile. "I'm cool I'll tell you about it when we leave out of the store."

Before they could get two feet out of the store Divine was on it. "Girl Promise asking can he spend Christmas with us."

"That's a good thing. He needs to spend the holidays with y'all maybe him seeing what he's missing would make him want to get some help."

Divine stopped to look at her, "Girl it's been a little over a year. You don't think he knows what he's missing by now. I would have thought he would have tried to come around for Treasure birthday but he didn't. I mean he missed his own biological child's birthday and now he thinks I'm going to let him come for Christmas. Fuck nawl. Only way he's going see my kids is if we're visiting him at a rehab. I told him that already. And seeing as though he hasn't checked himself in yet he won't be spending anytime with us, feeling us up with false hope."

By the time she finished ranting they were standing in front of the Nike store. She wanted to go in because she wanted to grab the kids some ACG boots but she just couldn't bring herself to open the door. And once the tears started coming down her face she turned and headed towards the car silently crying to herself.

By the time they made it in the car Cherokee was crying along with her.

With tears in her eyes she looked over at Cherokee and asked, "Now why the hell are you crying?"

She started laughing, "I don't know, you know I'm a cry baby and you can't cry around me."

Divine started crying even harder why she didn't know. All she knew was she wanted her Promise back. After hearing the two options she gave him over a year ago he left the house telling her he was cool and he could handle it. And she hasn't seen him ever since. Every now and then she receives a text from him telling her that he was sorry. She knew he was staying back at the condo but she refused to go see about him. If he missed her and the kids the way he said he did he would man the fuck up and check himself into a rehab. She didn't care that he was still handling his business in the streets. She didn't give a flying fuck that he was still the King of Kinsman County, functional or not she was not allowing him back into her life and her children's lives because she knew it would just be a matter of time before he was a full fledge junkie. She promised him over many texts that when he was ready she would be there for him every step of the way. But she guessed getting his life back in order and seeing his kids wasn't an option for him. Sometimes she felt that Innocence was letting him sneak over there to see the kids. Why wouldn't she he was her son and what other reason could it have been that he didn't care that he hasn't seen them in all this time. But she never questioned the kids about seeing their father and he must have trained them not to say if they have seen him. And she knew he still watched every move that she made so she made sure to tread lightly. Drugs or no drugs she knew she was still his.

Pulling out her phone she responded to his text.

Me: Don I know I may have been harsh with you about this situation but that's only because I want you to man up and snap out of this shit. But maybe if you knew how you were killing me you would try to seek help. Baby you're my heart and my king. Don I need you back in my life and back in the kids' lives. I miss waking up to the smell of you making breakfast for your family. I miss watching you roll around on the floor playing with the kids. Baby I miss snuggling up close to you at night. Do you realize I haven't had a good night's sleep since you've been gone? Don you're so focused on you that you forgot about me. How could you forget about your best friend, your lover, your Queen. Who would have ever thought you will leave your Queen unprotected. I never thought I would see the day.

Promise read over her text a thousand times and shed at least a tear every time he read it. He wanted to be strong but for some reason he just couldn't, he enjoyed the feeling that the heroin gave him. He kept trying to explain to her that his habit wasn't as bad as she thought, but she wasn't trying to listen to reason. Hell she had a habit of her own which was drinking, something that he only did on occasions. He only smoked weed when he was with his cousin but Sincere on the other hand blew trees day in and night out. That nigga couldn't go a whole two hours without blazing up. To him it didn't matter, a habit was a habit and they both were being hypercritical because they both had one. But it was all good because one thing he did know for sure was that even though he has lost his way in the world momentarily he knew he would always be **SINCERELY HERS.**

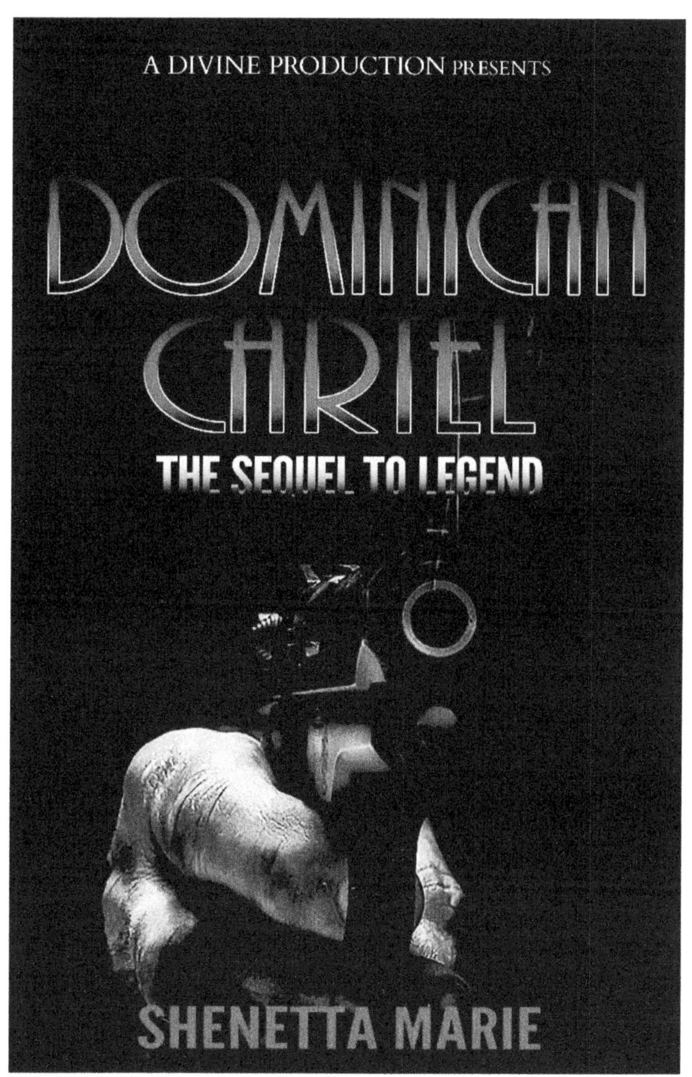
A DIVINE PRODUCTION PRESENTS
DOMINICAN
CARTEL
THE SEQUEL TO LEGEND
SHENETTA MARIE

In The Lab

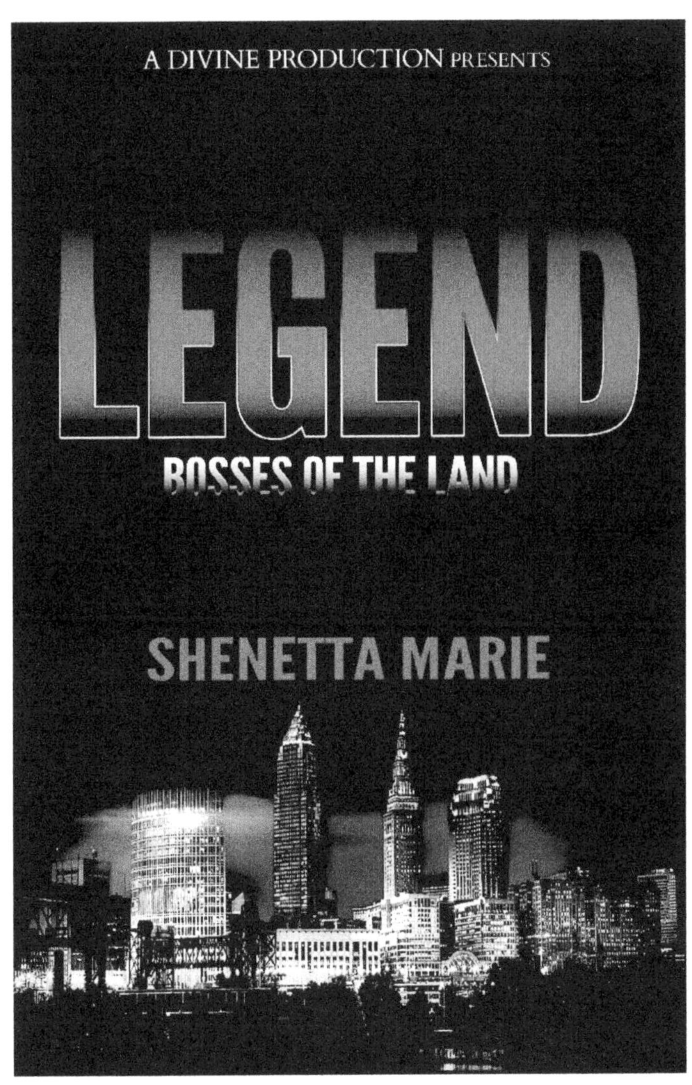

Available now

Available Now

About the Author

Shenetta Marie born and raised in Cleveland, Ohio, is a mother of two wonderful sons. She loves to spend time with her family and close friends and is now embracing her new love, writing.

Feel free to visit the rising Author/Publisher @
shenettamarie@yahoo.com
Follow her on twitter @shenettamarie
facebook Author Shenetta Marie
IG @shenettamarie

Made in the USA
Middletown, DE
24 March 2023

27053695R00136